He was lost. The thought sent a chill from his brain to his spinal column and down to his legs. He backed away from the skeletal trees, his legs feeling soft, his joints all awash on one another. The mist was thick and very close . . .

Something twittered on his left. Violently he turned right and ran. The mud splashed. It was getting darker. The ground was hard, then soft under his shoes. The mist clawed into his lungs and made the inside of his nostrils sting. He ran.

Then his hands snapped up just in time to keep him from crashing face first into a sudden rise of rock. As he gasped tiny, terrified breaths, he realized that he was at the bottom of a cliff. He turned his back to the wall and tried to keep his eyes closed and not to think; but they kept on opening and darting about of their own volition. Hysterically they tried to fix on some form in the dark haze.

Something was coming toward him.

THE TOWERS OF TORON

by
Samuel R. Delany

ace books
A Division of Charter Communications Inc.
A GROSSET & DUNLAP COMPANY
1120 Avenue of the Americas
New York, New York 10036

THE TOWERS OF TORON

An ACE Book

Printed in U.S.A.

Yes, Antoine, I was writing another novel.

Author's Note

Revising one's old fiction because of one's new ideas suggests a confusion of art and journalism—at any rate, a mistaken notion of the way art gains either effect or worth. Revising old fiction to clarify ideas now past creative ferment is a tricky business at best. Writers better than I have tried both and botched them.

Written between the end of 1961 and the beginning of 1964, each of the *Towers'* three books went into production practically as it was finished; by the time I was nearing the end of book two, book one was in type. But I had already made notes on changes I would have liked in volume one, particularly in the prologue, several of the vignettes in chapter one, and the expository material of chapter six. And, in chapter eight, I had invented a rather clumsy language for one of my subcultures which, by now, I realized, admitted no development. Because, however, no changes could be made, some preposterous robots were hauled on stage at the end of book two to explain (by exploding) some of the looser ends from book one. And a few incomprehensible grunts were strewn though book three in deference to that obstreperous tongue.

In 1966, for the British edition, I incorporated my notes, removed the robots, and from the rest excised some clumsy sentences of exposition, now superfluous, and the language.

That, essentially, is the version here.

I do whittle when I re-read, lopping an adjective here, pruning a prepositional phrase there, adjusting a bit of syntax elsewhere. Poets from Keats to Auden, in this way, have practically wrecked some of their best poems. But the *Towers* is prose. And I would hazard that, save the changes mentioned, chapter by chapter, paragraph by paragraph, sentence by sentence through ninety-eight percent of the work, the substance is one with the original edition.

And I suspect, with all its flaws and excesses, it is time to stop whittling.

—SAMUEL R. DELANY   *San Francisco, 1970*

CHAPTER ONE

ENGRAVED on a four by five card in graceful letters that leaned like dancers:

> *To Her Grace the Duchess of Petra*
> *You are invited to attend a ball at dawn*
> *Given by His Royal Highness*
> *King Uske*
> *to honour the patriotic efforts of*
> *Tildon Aquariums*
> *"We have an Enemy beyond the Barrier"*

Two things caught the eye about this invitation: first, "Tildon Aquariums" had been printed slightly lopsided in a type face a fraction different from the rest. Second, there was a ten-inch coil of wire taped to the lower righthand corner.

She tore loose the message coil, threaded it into the machine. On the screen dots of colour became the face of a blond young man with unhealthy features. "Well, there you are, dear cousin," it spoke with languid insolence. "You see, I'm attaching this personal entreaty with your invitation. Do come away from your little island to my big one. You were always my favourite cousin, and life has been passionately dull since you went into—what else can I call it—seclusion. Please, dearest Petra, come to my party and help us celebrate our coming victory. So much has happened— So much has happened— So much has happened—"

The Duchess made a disgusted sound, banged the shut-off button, and the face disintegrated. "A nick in the message wire," she said and looked up. "Is Tildon a subsidiary of your father's company, Jon?"

"It's one of the few left that isn't."

"I wonder how much Tildon gave him. My poor cousin really thinks he can seduce the money he needs to keep up the war by the promise of official parties given at the palace."

"Royal patronage still holds its magic, Petra. Your family has wielded power in Toromon for centuries, but my great-great grandfathers—and Tildon's— were farmers ploughing by hand on the mainland, or pulling their fish in over the edge of their rowboat. When the council decided that these parties should be given, it knew what it was doing."

She ran her fingers across the mother-of-pearl inlay on the desk. "We're such a disparate land. There are still people living like cavemen on the mainland; yet we have planes, scientists like your sister." She shook her head. "Don't people like your father, Tildon, and the others, realize they have the real power now? I have enough to live sumptuously here on this island, but I couldn't make more than a token gift to the war effort compared with what these industrial families can—assuming I would want to support the war in the first place.''

Jon smiled. ''Still, they want the Dukes and Barons to nod on them when they give. Not to mention the King.''

The Duchess looked at the invitation again. Suddenly her face twisted. ''He prints these by the thousands and just fills in the name of the next moneybag to be honoured, right on the dotted line. I'm afraid the thing that still upsets me more than anything else is the vulgarity.''

''But your family is the standard of good taste, Petra. That's what the rest of us have been taught all our lives.'' There was slight mockery in his voice.

She accepted it. ''Yes,'' and put down the card. ''We have been taught the same thing. But there must be some standards—even during a war.''

''Why? They're learning, Petra; my father and the others, they're beginning to learn just how much power they do have. After all, the war is being fought for them. As long as their products are used in the war, as long as those malcontent with life and Toromon can be funnelled into the war, everyone will stay happy and in his place. If the war stops, then the royal family—you topple.''

Petra spoke back shortly. ''As long as they are blind enough to seek royalty's favour, they are not fit to guide something as complex as Toromon. That's why I spirited off Prince Let to the mainland, so there would be someone with a sense of the scope of this country who would be safe to govern after these intrigues, working around us now, come full circle.''

Jon's face lost some of its cynicism. ''With the set up of the council and the government, Petra, the King can still hide much of his power. While it is hidden, no one can judge what it is. Is he a madman?

Or is he very, very clever?"

"He is my cousin. You were his schoolmate. What do you think?"

"There are great secrets involved in this war. But great secrets have kept the royal family in power since it established itself and set itself at the head of this chaotic fragment of the world."

The Duchess touched her fingers together, nodding. "My great-great-how-many-greats grandfathers with their ships looted the coasts, Jon Koshar, pillaged their neighbours' on these islands, using the fragmentary remains of the technology that survived the Great Fire. The radiation on the mainland stopped their expansion inland and the hot currents out from shore did the same. But when they were stopped, they decided that organized government could accomplish more efficiently what piracy had accomplished up till then. There's great variation over the land of Toromon, but it's bounded. They learned not to exhaust what lay within those boundaries, and became a line of Kings and Queens. Now the power is about to shift; but these others must learn the same thing."

"However your ancestors learned it, Petra, today people like Tildon and my father will pay exhorbitantly for your approval. Perhaps because they suspect what you know." Now Jon picked up the card. "Or perhaps because they are vain and ignorant. My father," he repeated, turning the card over. "His greatest disgrace was that I should offend the King and go to the penal mines for it. His greatest triumph was that the King himself should honour my sister when she came from the university with his royal presence at her ball. As long as these are the limits of his happiness, the King can get money for his war, and fill in the names on the dotted line."

"I wish I could allow myself such intellectual clumsiness." She lowered her chin to her finger tips.

Jon looked surprised.

"You call your hysterical murder merely an offence."

Jon clamped his jaw.

"And you have not spoken to your father since the 'offence' to find out exactly what he feels."

Jon's jaw unclamped and words started in his throat.

"And it is too easy for you to call your father, who was astute enough to build a fortune through brilliant, if unscrupulous, economic exploitation, a puppet of these petty vanities. No, attacking the problem this way leaves too many questions—"

"Petra!"

The Duchess looked up, surprised. She brushed her hand across the sunrise copper hair pulled back by a burnished cluster of gold sea-serpents, "I'm sorry, Jon," and her hand went out and took his. "We have all been here together too long. But when I see how my family, how my people can fool themselves, it hurts. There is a sense of decency that's like a barometer to a man's or a country's health. I don't know. Perhaps I'm too much in love with some idea of the aristocracy: I was born into it. I turned away from it when I was young. Now I find myself back in it again. I think we shall accept that invitation, Jon Koshar."

"I see," Jon said. "With Arkor as well?"

"Yes. The three of us will be needed again." She hesitated. "You were contacted by . . . them also, weren't you? The *Lord of the Flames*..."

Jon pushed his black hair back from his forehead. "Yes."

They turned at a sound behind them. Doors shaped

like double mollusk shells fanned apart. In the doorway stood the giant seven feet and a handful of inches tall. On the left side of his face three scars jagged down his cheek and neck, darker parallel welts in dark skin. "When will we leave?" Arkor asked. The triplex of scars was the brand with which the frequent telepaths among the tall, mainland forest people were marked.

"Tonight," Petra said.

"You're going to take Tel and Alter," said Arkor. It was a statement, not a question.

Jon frowned. "Are you, Petra?"

"We're all going to pay my cousin the King a visit," she told them. "We've received warning. The *Lord of the Flames* is loose somewhere on earth once more."

"We drove him across the universe three years ago," Jon said.

"We may have to do it again."

Across the evening salmon-coloured clouds strung out like floating hair. Red light caught on the polished brass that ran around the yacht deck. Water flopped at the side of the boat. "Everyone's aboard," Jon told the Duchess.

"Then we can start." She turned and issued an order. Engines rang out like plucked cords on a musical instrument. The ship mounted, then plunged forward towards the night. As blackness washed the sky and stars stuck diamond-tipped pins into evening, Jon and Petra lingered at the rail. "Somewhere out there is the war. In which direction?" she asked.

"Who knows?" Jon motioned towards the horizon. "Somewhere beyond the radiation barrier, somewhere out in the mist of our planet."

One of the motormen cried out from the yacht bridge. "Toron ahead!"

"We're nearly there," said Petra. They looked over the prow of the ship, across the water.

Imagine a black gloved hand, ringed with myriad diamonds, amethysts by the score, turquoises, rubies. Now imagine this glittering hand rising slowly above the midnight horizon, each jewel with its internal flame. Thus the island of Toron thrust over the edge of the sea.

The windows of the Grand Ballroom in the royal palace of Toron rose coffin-shaped two stories towards the ceiling. As the panes lightened, the musicians blew windy music from their tuned sea-shells, and above the marine chords, the weaving voice of a theremin dipped and climbed. Emerald and coral gauze swirled from the women's arms, purple and crimson on the jackets of the men.

Through the wide windows, against the ending night, the dark band of the transit-ribbon leapt away from the laboratory tower of the palace and disappeared among the other towers of the City till at last it soared over the sea, over the mainland beach, over the forest of lush titan-palms and descendants of the oak trees of an earth five hundred years in the past, across the penal mines where men and women prisoners toiled the metal tetron from shafts sunk in the twisted rock, across groved plains where only in the past three years had vegetation dared creep, and at last into the mainland city of Telphar. Telphar!—in the past three years it had been converted into the strongest military establishment earth had ever seen, or so her generals boasted.

"A ball in the morning!" the young girl in the ruby

silk exclaimed. The shoulder of her dress was fastened with a copper lobster whose beaten tail curved to cover her right breast. "Don't you think this is a wonderful idea, to have a ball at dawn?"

The elderly woman beside her pulled her thin lips tighter. "How ridiculous," she said softly. "I remember when balls were affairs of taste and breeding." A caterer passed them offering hors d'oeuvres. "Just look," the woman continued. On her head she wore a silver wig coiled through with rope pearls. "Just look at that!" Strips of fillet were wound about the toasted circlets. "That fish came from the aquariums! Fish from the aquariums served at an affair of state! Why I remember when no one would think of serving anything but imported goods from the mainland. Aquarium grown fish! Why, the idea. What has the world come to?"

"I never could tell the difference between one and the other anyway," the girl in the ruby dress replied, munching into a paté of fish-roe and chopped scallion.

The woman with the silver wig *humphed*.

Jon Koshar moved away and wandered through the hall, over the polished white stone that shimmered with the reflections of fabulous gowns. Isolated on one side of the room and swathed in fur were two representatives of the forest guards, the lonely giants of Toromon's great forest on the mainland. A few feet away stood three squat ambassadors from the neo-neanderthal tribes. They wore bronze wrist bands and leather skirts. Across the floor people clustered around the honoured representatives of Tildon's aquarium. Yes, three years ago it would have been different. But now—

Someone screamed.

Jon whirled round as the scream again crossed the ballroom. Heads turned, people crowded forward on one another, then pushed back. Jon was shoved sideways and someone put an elbow in his chest. More people screamed, backing away from what staggered over the ballroom floor.

Something inside that had always made him go against crowds took him forward, and suddenly he was at the edge of the clearing. An elderly man in a bright red suit was lurching across the floor, his hands against his eyes. Behind him a scarlet cape billowed, sagged about his ankles, then billowed once more as he fell forward.

Sticky crimson bubbled between his fingers and dribbled down the backs of his hands staining his scarlet cuffs darker. He cried out again, and suddenly the scream turned into liquid gurgling.

The man went down on one knee. When he came up, there was a smear over the stone and the knee of the trouser leg had deepened to maroon.

Another figure had detached himself from the crowd, slim, blond, dressed in white. Jon recognized the King.

The scarlet figure splattered to the floor at His Majesty's feet and rolled over, his grasping hands falling from his face.

Now more people cried out and even Jon gasped in a breath and bit down on it like metal.

Blood puddled from both cuffs and trouser legs. Red jelly slipped away from what had been a face. Suddenly the barrel chest collapsed and the red cloth that had covered flesh now sagged down till it draped no more than the spikes of meatless ribs. One hand raised two inches from where it lay on the bloody cape, then fell back, tarsals and metatarsals separating, a scattering of tiny bones, as the radial tendon dissolved. At the same time, the skull rolled away from the neck: cheek bone, nasal cartilege, and chin chuckled over the floor.

Through the crowd across from him Jon saw the red-headed figure of the Duchess moving towards the arched ballroom entrance. Immediately Jon turned, made his way to the edge of the room, and in three minutes had skirted the floor to the entrance where the Duchess was waiting. She seized his shoulder. "Jon," she whispered, "do you know who that was? Do you know?"

"I know how it was done," he volunteered. "But not who."

"That was Prime Minister Chargill, the head of the Council." She took a breath. "All right. Now you tell me how."

"When I was in prison at the mines," Jon said, "a not too close friend of mine was an expert toxologist, and sometimes he used to shoot off his mouth. That was terenide. It's an enzyme action cellular tranquilizer."

"You mean the body cells get so tranquil they can't even hold on to one another?"

"That's about it," Jon said. "The results are what you saw happen to Chargill."

The music, which had stopped, suddenly resumed, and above the twining melodies a casual voice sounded over a loud-speaker system: "Ladies and gentlemen, I am so sorry that this unpleasantry has interrupted my morning party, so terribly sorry. I must request you all, however, to repair to your homes. Our orchestra will now play for us the Victory Anthem of Toromon." The melody on the theremin halted abruptly, then plunged into the soaring theme of the Victory Anthem.

"Come up to my suite immediately," whispered the Duchess to Jon. "There's something I wanted you to see before this. Now it's imperative."

Across the room, the first light strained the panes in the immense coffin-shaped windows. Like violet blades, light slanted through the room, over the heads of the scurrying guests avoiding the scarlet horror drying on the dancing floor.

Jon and Petra hurried through the arched door-way.

The Duchess Petra had secured a family suite among the personal chambers of the palace. A few minutes after they left the ballroom, she ushered Jon through the triple door into the softly lit, purple carpeted room. "Jon," she said as they stepped inside, "this Rolth Catham. Rolth Catham, this Jon Koshar, whom I told you about."

Jon had stopped at the door, his hand half extended, looking at the . . . the man in the chair. He wanted to close his eyes and rub them, but what he saw was not going to go away. Half of Catham's face was transparent. Part of his skull had been replaced with a plastic case. Through it Jon could see blood boiling along the net of artificial capillaries; metal teeth studded a plastic jaw bone, and above that an eyeball hovered before the ghostly grey convolutions of brain, half hidden by a web of vessels.

Jon's mind thawed from the first surprise, and he said out loud, "Catham. Catham of Catham's *Revised History of Toromon.*" He jumped at the first familiar thought in his mind, turning it into a pleasantry to battle the surprise. "We used your book in school."

The three-quarters of Catham's mouth that was flesh smiled. "And your name is Koshar? Is there any connection between you and Koshar Aquariums or Koshar Hydroponics? Or for that matter with Dr. Koshar who discovered the inverse subtrigonometric functions and applied them to the random system of spacial co-ordinates—which is more or less the technological reason behind the present conflict in which Toromon has got itself engaged?"

"Koshar Aquariums and Hydroponics are my father. Dr. Koshar is my sister."

Catham's mobile eyebrow raised.

"I told both of you before that I would have surprises for you," the Duchess said. "Professor Catham, we're going to exchange stories this evening. Just a moment. Arkor!" the Duchess called.

In the silence following, Professor Catham caught Jon staring at his glittering visage. The three-quarter smile came again. "I usually announce right off when I meet someone for the first time that I was in an accident fifteen years ago, a freak explosion out at University Island. I'm one of General Medical's more successful, if a trifle bizarre experiments."

"I assumed it was something like that," Jon said. "I was just remembering once when I was in the prison mines. There was an accident and a buddy of mine got one side of his face smashed in. Only General Medical was far away, and the medical facilities out there were never particularly famous anyway. He died."

"I see," said Professor Catham. "That must have been the mine disaster of '79. Did they do anything about the safety conditions after that?"

"Not while I was there," Jon said. "I went into prison when I was eighteen and the tetron explosion was in my first year. Five years . . . later, when I got out, they hadn't even changed the faulty cutter machinery."

Just then a door in the side of the room opened and Arkor came in.

At the sight of the triple scars that branded the giant's neck, the historian's eyebrow raised once more. "Do you always keep a telepath in your service, Your Grace?"

"Arkor is not in my service," the Dutchess said. "Nor are we in his. Professor, this is very important. Not twenty minutes ago Prime Minister Chargill was assassinated. I'd like you to go over what you told me when I spoke to you earlier."

"Chargill . . . ?" began the historian. The eyebrow drew down where the other would have met it in a frown. "Assassinated?" Then the half-face relaxed again. "Well, it's either the malis who are responsible, or perhaps the council itself wanted him out of the way . . ."

"Please, Professor," said the Duchess. "Will you repeat what you told me before. Then we'll add what we can."

"Oh, yes," Catham said. "Oh, yes. Well, I was telling Her Grace when she first called me at the University, or rather ferreted me out of . . . Well, anyway." He looked from Jon to Arkor, to Petra, and back. "Anyway," he went on. "Toromon is perhaps the strangest empire in the history of Earth. You have lived in it all your lives so its unique properties do not strike you, but to one who has studied the development of the world before the Great Fire, five hundred years ago, its uniqueness becomes apparent. Toromon's empire consists of the island of Toron, the handful of islands scattered near it, and the fifteen hundred or so square miles of mainland opposite the islands, that of a strip of beach, followed by meadow lands, followed by forests, followed by an uninhabitable rocky crescent that more or less cuts off this fifteen hundred square miles from the rest of the mainland continent, which is still hopelessly radioactive. After the Great Fire, this area I've outlined was completely isolated from the rest of the world by radioactive land and radioactive currents in the sea. Until recently, we never thought that there was anything left on earth to be cut off from. There were several good technical libraries that survived, and some of our ancestors fortunately were literate, educated people, so we have a fairly good picture of what the world was like before the Great Fire. And although there was economic and social back-sliding at first, when a balance was finally achieved, technology began to progess once more and within a comparatively short time, it had equalled that of before the Great Fire, and in many non-destructive areas, surpassed it. Very early in our history, we discovered the metal tetron as a source of power, the one major factor that our pre-Great Fire ancestors seemed entirely ignorant of, from the records we have.

"Now what is unique about Toron is this. No empire that we know of before the Great Fire ever survived for over a hundred years in complete isolation from any disruptive force. Nor did any empire, country, or even tribe that was in isolation ever develop once it had been isolated.

"Yet through the strange set of circumstances I have outlined—the surviving libraries, the intelligence of our ancestors, the geographical diversity of our land allowing for interchange between rural and urban cultural patterns—Toromon has existed for half a thousand years alone while still managing to preserve a constantly developing technology. The details of this process are fascinating, and I have devoted most of my life to their study, but that is not what I want to explore now.

"The effect of this situation, however, is like a thermite reaction going on inside a sealed bottle. It doesn't matter how long it takes, eventually the bottle will explode. And the longer the bottle remains sealed, the further the fragments will fly. And, that explosion has taken place." Catham leaned forward in his chair now and brought his fingers meshing together like the tines of fork. "Sixty-five years ago Toromon's scientists conducted the first experiments in matter transmission. The transit-ribbon was built between Telphar, our one city on the mainland, and Toron, our island Capitol. Then Telphar was cut off from us by an increase in the radiation barrier— almost as if the area of Toromon's empire were being diminished to hasten the final explosion. Three years ago we learned that a group of forest people, probably controlled by the enemy had managed to increase the radiation artificially, using some equipment from Telphar itself." Catham turned to Jon now. "Three years ago, as well, your sister, Dr. Clea Koshar, discovered the inverse subtrigonometric functions and their application to the random system of special co-ordinates. In six months the old transit-ribbon was turned into an antenna that could beam matter wherever we wished, and Telphar, inhabitable again, became a military establishment to send men by the thousand to any place on the globe." Catham raised one hand to his transparent cheek. "And the war continues. Why a war? Why not peace? Toromon has been too long held in. That's all I know.''

''I thought you would mention what I saw as the most obvious thing about all of this,'' the Duchess said. ''Dr. Catham, do you remember the incident that caused war to be declared three years ago?''

''Yes. The King's younger brother, Prince Let, was kidnapped. That must have been done by some early group of malcontents. The malis go back quite a way, but they were never as strong as they are now. All they actually accomplish is stirring up trouble. Some people think they are connected with the enemy. And no one, so I hear, will even walk through the Devil's Pot after dark.''

''It was never a particularly savoury area of the City,'' replied the Duchess. ''But Professor Catham, now I'm going to tell you my story. It's a lot briefer than yours, and more incredible. But it's true. Toromon has had access to matter-transmission on a large scale for three years. There are at least two other races in the universe that have had access to it for billions. They use it to travel among the stars. These races aren't even composed of individuals, but are rather collective consciousnesses. Their method of interstellar travel is more psychic than physical. One seems to be a sort of amoral experimentor. The other, much older, race is benevolent and composed of three centres of consciousness, rather than one, which seem to check and balance one another. We call it the Triple Being.

''You spoke of Toromon's uniqueness, its combination of isolation and development. The experimentor, whom we call the *Lord of the Flames,* was aware of Toromon uniqueness, and from the outside he began to meddle in order to keep it isolated as long as possible. You wonder where the rebels got the equipment and knowledge to close the radiation barrier? It was from the *Lord of the Flames*.

"Myself, Jon, and Arkor here were contacted by the Triple Being three years ago. With their help we rooted out the agent of the *Lord of the Flames*, though too late to stop the major explosion. But he's back again, Professor Catham. What the results of his presence will be this time we don't know. The kidnapping of Prince Let was our doing. For the past three years he's been safely with the forest guards on the mainland. We hope that eventually this hysterical war will end, and then Prince Let can come back and perhaps straighten out whatever's left of Toromon, if there is anything. While he was in the palace with his mother and brother, his very life and sanity were in danger. It was all we could do."

"I see," said Catham. "And you're going to prove all this? Why tell me about it in the first place?"

"Because we need someone with a historical orientation to help us and advise. The Triple Being will only help so much in order not to upset our culture by introducing extraneous upsetting elements. The first advice we need is what to do with two youngsters who helped us in our first effort, a boy and a girl. The boy, Tel, ran away from a small fishing village on the mainland to Toron when he got involved with us. The girl is an acrobat. They were very helpful to us then, but we don't need them any more, and it seems a shame to keep them away from society this long. But they have a tremendous amount of information that might be dangerous, especially to themselves. And there's one more problem." She turned to Arkor. "Bring the children in, will you?"

Arkor turned from the room. He came back followed by a boy of about seventeen with dark skin and sea-green eyes. After the boy came a girl perhaps a year older and nearly an inch taller. Her skin was tanned the same as the boy's, but her hair was the colour and texture of bleached silk. Both looked surprised at the apparition that was Catham, but they were silent.

"The special problem is this," the Duchess told him, and reached for a button on the arm of her chair. At her touch, the lights in the room dimmed to half their original brightness.

Rolth Catham started forward in his seat. He was sitting alone in the purple carpeted room—with five empty, but animated suits of clothes, a woman's sitting in the Duchess's chair, two men's standing beside it, and the scant garb of the two youngsters hovering by the door. But though the lights were dim, they were still bright enough to see that the bodies inhabiting them had disappeared.

From the chair the Duchess's voice, natural and unruffled, continued. "During the time we were first involved in this affair, the Triple Being went as far as to make us immune to certain frequencies of radiation by re-structuring our crystallization matrix. The side effect, however, was that the index of refraction of our bodies' substance took a nose dive. Which means that when the light gets below a certain intensity, we disappear . . ." The light went up, and the five people were back in the room. "So you see the problem. That demonstration, incidentally, is our only real proof."

"I'm impressed," Catham said. "No, I don't believe you. But I will take it on as a theoretical problem, which might be fun to work on. You want to know what to do with the youngsters? Spray them with pigmented viva-foam, General Medical developed it for me—but I'm not vain enough to wear it. Turn them out on the world, and leave them to their own devices. The remaining three of you concentrate on the *Lord of the Flames*." Catham rose. "You can contact me back at the University. I must say it's all very interesting. But I seriously don't believe it's anything more than a psychotic fantasy on your part." He smiled his three-quarter smile. "And that's a shame, Your Grace, because you have a terribly vivid imagination. But I will advise you to the best of my ability, however I can." He stopped. "Consider this before I go. You say you're responsible for the kidnapping of Prince Let three years ago? The government finally decided it was malis. Malis probably are responsible for Chargill's death—if he is dead. In your fantasy world, aren't you perhaps responsible for that?" Catham went to the door, opened it, seemed surprised to find it not locked, and went out.

Arkor, Jon, and the Duchess looked at one another.

"Well," said Arkor. "He is serious about advising us, but he doesn't believe it."

"That's better than nothing," Jon said.

"Arkor find out what in the world viva-foam is, and get hold of some as soon as possible," the Duchess said.

CHAPTER TWO

FIFTEEN COPPER centi-units, on top of an empty cardboard crate, had been arranged into a square—minus one corner.

A hairy fist whammed the surface, the coins leapt, and the three men who had been kneeling around the box fell backwards spluttering. "What's the idea?" demanded one with curly brown hair.

"Hey! Hey, you look at me!" A grin slashed the wide face of the interrupter. Squat, barrel-broad, with no neck and little chin, he had hair and eyebrows the colour of unravelled hemp. "Look at me!" he bellowed again, threw back his head, and laughed.

"Aw, cut it out," whined the green-eyed, heavily freckled kid they called Shrimp. "Why don't you pick on someone your own size?"

Lug's squat torso rolled back on his pelvis and his brachydactylic hands slapped at his low, heavy stomach. "I pick on . . ." He turned to the third man. ". . . you!"

Waggon, the third around the crate, had the same

thick physique, only his hair was wiry and black and his forehead even lower.

"Aw, leave Waggon alone," Shrimp complained. "We're trying to teach him to play a game."

"He's my size," grunted Lug, giving Waggon a playful whack on the shoulder.

Waggon, who had been concentrating on the coins, looked up surprised, his wide eyes blinking. Very little white showed around his pupils.

"Leave him alone, Lug," Shrimp said again.

A second time Lug belted Waggon's shoulder. Suddenly Waggon rolled to his feet, ropes of muscle knotting along his shoulders and thighs. He leapt, and they tumbled to the floor. The other recruits looked up from their bunks or where they sat reading military pamphlets. One seven foot forest guard who had been leaning by the double-decker bed peeled himself from the olive drab wall, and walked towards the two scuffling neanderthals. Suddenly he reached for them. There was a howl, another howl, and then Waggon and Lug were dangling by their collars from the forest guard's fists. "Why don't you apes learn to do a passable imitation of human beings?" the guard asked in a resonable voice.

Big-pupilled eyes blinked, fists folded like cats' paws, and the big toes sticking through the open-toed boots curled in. The forest guard let go, and they bounced to the floor, catching themselves on their knuckles. They shook themselves and lumbered off, at once seeming to have forgotten the incident.

"Watch it," came a voice from the door.

Everyone snapped erect as the officer entered, followed by three new recruits: a forest guard with a shaved skull, a dark-skinned black-haired boy about seventeen with vivid sea-green eyes, and an unusually squat neanderthal who kept blinking.

"New men here," the officer said. "Watch it! Ptorn 047 AA-F." The shaved guard stepped forward. "Tel 211 BQ-T." Tel, green-eyed and silent, stepped forward. "Kog 019 N-H." The blinking neanderthal moved up now. "All right, you guys," the officer said, "don't forget there's an orientation meeting in . . ." He looked at the ceiling chronometer. ". . . eleven minutes. When that gong sounds, hustle!" He left the room.

The three newcomers tried to smile as half a dozen men called out a perfunctory, "Hello."

Green-eyed and freckled Shrimp came over. "Hey, any of you fellows interested in a game of chance? Why don't you come over with me and get to know some of the guys. My name is Archibald Squash. Really. Imagine a mother naming a kid Archibald. But you can call me Shrimp." He seemed to be directing his attention more and more towards the neanderthal. Now he turned directly to him and said. "Your name is Kog, right? Well, come on over and join the game."

Tel and Ptorn looked at each other, then followed Shrimp and Kog to where another man was arranging coins on top of the cardboard crate.

"Hi, Curly," Shrimp said. "This Kog. Kog, Curly. Kog wants to play a little game with us, Curly. That right, Kog?" His enthusiastic friendliness seemed forced to Tel. But the neanderthal grinned and nodded. "You just sit down here," and Shrimp, his hand on Kog's shoulder, pushed him to a squat beside the crate. "Now this is the way we play—you got any money?—you arrange the coins in a square, four by four, but with one corner missing. Then you take this here deci-unit and just flip it across the

box-top so that it hits the corner, see? And two coins
fly off the far edges of the square, like that. Now we
number the coins on the far side—one, two, three,
four, five, six, seven. (Get your money out, Kog) and
you bet on two of them. Let me show you. I bet on
two and six. Now I flip the coin and . . . two and five
fly off. Here, you get half a unit. That's 'cause only
half my bet came in." He placed a half-unit piece in
Kog's hand. "Now. You want to try."

"Eh . . . yeah." Kog nodded. "What do you call
this?"

"Randomax, randy, double-dice, cut-coin,
seven-down, take your pick."

"Randy . . . ?" Kog asked.

"Randy," repeated Shrimp. "All right. Now put
your money down. Fine. Your bet?"

"Huh? Oh. Eh . . . two and six."

Kog flipped, the coin struck the vacant corner, and
two coins that were neither two nor six flew from the
edge.

Shrimp made a regretful sound and Curly picked
up Kog's unit note.

"Huh?" asked the neanderthal.

"Oh, it's not over," Shrimp said. "That's just a
first try. Now we all go again."

Crumpled notes landed on the box-top and the coin
was flipped again; then again; and then again.

A bewildered frown had chiselled itself into Kog's
face when suddenly Ptorn, the smooth-skulled forest
guard, leaned over the makeshift table and said
levelly, "How about giving me a chance at that?"

Shrimp looked up, at first surprised, then uneasy.
"I was just gonna suggest we broke up the game. I
mean . . ."

"Come on," insisted Ptorn. His long arm reached

across Tel's shoulder and his brown fingers squared the coins. Shrimp and Curly exchanged worried looks.

"Money," Ptorn said and put a unit note beside the coins.

Curly said, "I think I'll throw in my rag right now . . ." From around the box Shrimp kicked him and Curly's hand which had started leisurely for his winnings jerked back like a lengthened spring released.

"Three and five," Ptorn said. His wide ivory yellow index nails struck the milled edge.

Three and five leapt away from the square.

Ptorn picked up the money. "Two and six," he said, moving the corner coin back for another shot.

Click-click.

Two and six shot away.

Again Ptorn crumpled unit notes in his fingers. "Two and four."

"Now wait a minute . . ." Shrimp interrupted.

"Two and four."

Click-click.

He waited while they placed the final bills in his double width palm. Then he dropped the money in front of Kog. "This is yours, ape," he said, and walked away.

Shrimp sucked air between his teeth. "Them god damn big boys," he muttered looking after the guard. "How do they do it, huh? How? It's a perfectly fair game, but they win it every time." Suddenly he looked directly at Tel and smiled. "Hey," he said. "I bet you're from one of the mainland fishing villages."

"That's right," Tel said, smiling back. "How did you know?"

"Your eyes," Shrimp said. "Green. Like mine.

You know, us fishermen got to stick together. What made you hitch up with the army?''

Tel shrugged. ''Nothing else to do.''

''That's the truth,'' Shrimp said. ''Oh, this here is Curly, my partner in crime. He's a farmboy.''

Curly was still brooding over his randomax losses. ''I'm no farmboy,'' he grunted. ''I ran with a mali gang in the Devil's Pot for almost a year.''

''Sure, sure,'' Shrimp said. ''You know, this *is* a perfectly honest game. On His Majesty's yellow locks, I swear. But somehow. . .''

A gong broke the air like china and a metallic voice hit their ears: ''All new recruits report to the Stadium of the Stars. All new recruits report to the Stadium of the Stars . . .''

''That's us,'' Shrimp said, and with the others he and Tel, Curly behind them, started for the door.

Among the central buildings of Telphar to which the activity of the recruits was restricted was one structure that sank into the city like an inverted blister. Large enough to hold ten thousand beneath its canopy of flood-light simulated constellations, only one section was filled with restless, rangey soldiers.

On the dais glinting officers looked like toys. One approached the microphone, coughed into it, and as the echo staggered from wall to wall through the arena, he began: ''We have an enemy beyond the barrier, so hostile and abominable to every principle that mankind...''

Among the six hundred new soldiers, Tel sat, and listened, with more questioning than some, and not as much as others.

Then there was free time for the recruits until the next day when they would move to training headquarters. Tel still tagged after Shrimp and Curly.

"How does that game really work?" he finally asked when they were walking back to the barracks over the raised highway.

Shrimp shrugged. "Actually I don't exactly know. But somehow, the apes just don't have a chance. Oh, it's honest. But they just don't seem to win more than one out of ten. Regular people like you and me, well, we do all right and get better with practice. But those big guys . . . just forget it when they're around. Aren't you coming inside with us?"

They'd stopped at the barracks doors. "Naw," Tel said. "I think I'm going to keep walking and see what's around."

"I can tell you it's not much," Shrimp said. "But suit yourself. See you later."

As Tel went off, Shrimp started in, but Curly looked after the figure disappearing down the twilit roadway.

"What are you waiting for?" Shrimp asked.

"Shrimp, what colour are the kid's eyes?"

"Green," Shrimp said. "A little darker than mine."

"That's what I thought too, this afternoon. But I was looking at them all the way back here, and they're not any more."

"What colour are they then?"

"That's just it," Curly said. "They're not nothing. They're just like he's got two holes in his head."

"Hell, it's halfway dark. You just couldn't see."

"Oh yes I could. And I swear there wasn't a thing behind his eyelids. Just holes."

"This evening air's no good for you, boy," Shrimp said, shaking his head. "Come on inside and I'll play you an honest game of randy."

Tel wandered up the darkening roadway. He took a covered ramp that mounted from one spiralling highway to the next and came out above most of the surrounding buildings. Only the central palace was noticeably higher than this one. As the roadway wound round the dark tower, he could look across the triple railing over the smaller buildings of Telphar.

Below, the city stretched towards the plains, and the plains toward the mountains which still flickered faintly from the radiation barrier along their snaggled edge. It was all familiar to him. Mercury lights suddenly flicked on and bleached away the shadows on the ramp. Looking up, he saw a figure perhaps twenty yards away, another recruit out exploring.

As Tel approached, he realised the man was shaved bald. Then, coming closer, he recognized the forest guard who had arrived with him that afternoon.

Ptorn saw him and waved. "How you doing?"

"Fine," Tel said. "You just out walking too?"

Ptorn nodded and looked back over the railing. Tel stopped beside him and leaned on the top bar. A breeze pulled their sleeves back from their wrists and tugged at their open collars. "Hey," Tel said after a minute. "How did you work that thing with the randomax game?"

"You wouldn't understand.

"Huh?" said Tel. "Sure I would. Try me."

Ptorn turned sideways against the railing. "If you really want to know, try and follow this: suppose you're in the City, in Toron, and you're on the sidewalk. Now let's say one of those big trucks Koshar Hydroponics uses to ship stuff from the docks to the

warehouses is coming down the street. And let's say
it stops about a quarter of the way from the end of the
block. What happens?''

''It stops?''

''Well, no, I don't mean stop exactly. Let's say it
just cuts its motor.''

''Then it goes on rolling.''

''How far?''

Tel shrugged. ''That depends, doesn't it, on how
heavy the truck was, or how fast it was going?''

''Right,'' Ptorn said. ''But if you were crossing the
street, you could judge pretty accurately whether
you'd have time to get over, or even just about where
the truck would stop—once you saw it start to slow
down.''

''I guess so,'' Tel said.

''Well, do you realise that when you do that,
you're doing subconsciously a problem that would
take a mathematician with pencil and paper who
knew the exact weight of the truck, speed, rate of
deceleration, and friction component of the wheels at
least a couple of minutes to solve? Yet you do it in
under half a second with only the inaccurate information your senses can gather in a moment or two.''

Tel smiled. ''Yeah, that's pretty amazing. But
what's that got to do with the game?''

''Just this. You and I can do that. But if you put one
of the apes on that street corner, he'd have to stand
there until the truck came to a dead stop before he'd
dare cross over. Oh sure, if you taught him the mathematics and gave him a pencil, paper, and all the
factors, he could figure it out in about the same time
any other mathematician could. But he couldn't just
glance at the decelerating truck and figure where it
would stop.''

''I still don't quite see,'' Tel said.

"Well look: the way you men can just figure out by looking at things that the apes could never perceive, we can figure out things with just a glance that you men couldn't see either, like what angle and how hard to shoot that coin to make the ones we want to fly off the edges of the randomax square. If you can judge the direction and the velocity of the coin, you can figure the give and play of forces in the matrix and how it'll work out by the edge."

"I think I understand," said Tel.

"I can't explain the mathematics to you, but you can't explain the mathematics of your slowing truck to me."

"I guess not," Tel said. Suddenly he looked up at the forest guard and frowned. "You know when you said 'men' just before, you made it sound like something that . . . wasn't you."

Ptorn laughed. "What do you mean? The apes are part of you just like you men are part of us . . ."

"There," Tel said. "Even just now. Can't you hear the way you say it?"

Ptorn was quiet a moment. Then he said, "Yes. I hear it."

And the quietness suddenly repelled the youngster. "About the game," he said. "Could any of . . . us men, do what you did just guessing?"

Ptorn shrugged. "I suppose some exceptional minds among you can. But it's really not important, is it?"

"I guess not," Tel said. "Us men," he repeated. "What do you call yourselves, if you don't think of yourselves as men?"

Again Ptorn shrugged. "We think of ourselves as guards, forest guards. Only the 'forest' isn't so important."

"That's right. Sometimes you're referred to as

forest guards, sometimes as forest people.''

"As 'guards' we guard your penal mines at the edge of the forest and return escaped prisoners.''

"Oh yes,'' Tel said. "I'd forgotten.'' Again he looked over the dark buildings. "I knew an escaped prisoner once, before I joined the army.'' He was quiet for a moment.

"What are you thinking about?'' Ptorn asked.

"Huh?'' said Tel, looking up again. "Oh. As a matter of fact I'm thinking about a necklace.''

"A necklace?''

"Yeah,'' Tel said. "It was made of shells, polished shells that I strung on leather thongs.''

"What's that got to do with the escaped prisoner?''

"The girl I gave it to knew the prisoner too. It got broken once, stepped on. But I fixed it later. It was a pretty necklace. I polished the shells myself.''

"Oh,'' Ptorn said, a little softly, a little gently.

"What do you suppose all those lights are, way over there at the edge of the City?'' Tel asked.

"I'm not sure. Maybe they have something to do with the basic training camp. That looks like it's out in the restricted part of the City, though.''

"Yeah,'' said Tel. "But then why would they have lights on if there weren't any people there?''

"Who knows.'' Suddenly he stood straighter. "Hey, look.''

"What is it?'' Tel asked.

"Can you see? Some of them are going off, just flicking out.''

"Oh yeah, I just saw one. I wonder how far away they are?''

"I'm not sure,'' Ptorn said. "The ones that go out aren't coming on again. I wonder what it might have to do with basic training. You know it's supposed to be a pretty tough six weeks.''

. "I hear it's rough."

"Yeah," said Ptorn. "But so is the enemy.

"You know," said Tel, hunching his shoulders, "I haven't seen any of . . .you guards in the recruits who can read minds, the ones with the triple scars."

Ptorn stood up from the rail. "Really?" he said. "What do you know about the telepaths?"

"Nothing," Tel said. "I just know . . ." He stopped. "Well, I knew a guy once, I mean a guard, who could read minds. And he'd been scarred . . ."

"You know a lot of interesting people, don't you," Ptorn said. "Did you know that very few of you men know about the telepathic guards? Very, very few. In fact I'd say there were only about forty outside the forest who knew. Most of them are on the council."

"You're . . . not a telepath?" Tel asked.

Ptorn shook his head. "No. I'm not. And you're right. There're none in the army. They don't draft any."

"I don't usually talk about them," Tel said, warily.

"I think that's good," said Ptorn. "That's good." Suddenly he put his hand on Tel's shoulder. "Come on back to the barracks with me, boy. I want to tell you a story."

"About what?"

"About a prisoner. I mean about an escaped prisoner."

"Huh?"

They left the railing and walked towards the ramp that would take them back to barracks level. "I used to live near the penal mines, Tel. Not all of the forest patrolled the mines, but if you were born near them, chances are you would. We're organized there into squadrons, platoons, a miniature army. Further away the tribes of guards are much more informal, but near the mines where there's a job to do they have to be fairly strict. The guy in charge of our platoon was a quiet guard, with three scars banding his cheek and neck. We would sit around the campfire, talking or wrestling, but Roq—that was his name—would stand against a tree and watch. At the time I speak of, it had just got dark, and the sticks on which we had roasted our meat still leaned against the rock-rimmed fireplace, their tips shiny with grease. I could feel rain in the air hanging behind the still leaves.

"Then a branch snapped, leaves brushed one another, and Larta entered the clearing. Larta was a lieutenant in Frol's platoon that patrolled the woods a mile away. The left side of her face was also run with triple scars. She pushed a black pelt from her shoulder so that the swinging fur shimmered with orange firelight. Silently she and Roq conversed for perhaps ten seconds. Then, still without looking at the rest of us, they spoke so we would understand. 'When will they try to escape the mine?' she asked.

" 'Just before dawn,' Roq said.

"We all listened now.

" 'How many will try to run?' asked Roq.

" 'Three,' said Larta. 'There is the old man with the limp. He has been at the mines fourteen years. His right leg was smashed in the cave-in five years ago. He holds hate in his brain like a polished ruby, flickering behind his eyes. He is crouching beside the guard-house steps, rolling a twig between his fingers while he waits, trying not to think of the pain in his leg. He feels very old. Beside him is the heavy one. The texture of his mind is like iron and mercury. He is very conscious of his body, and as he crouches, he is thinking of the roll of fat where his legs bend at his waist and his stomach rolls across itself under his prison uniform. He is conscious of the six freckles on his right cheek and the ten on his left. There is an appendectomy scar across the right side of his belly, and he thinks of that now, briefly seeing the white walls of the General Medical building with their chrome handles. He has always tried to give the appearance of an easy, adaptable person around the prison camp, flowing quietly and precisely into the few new situations that arise. But the determination with which he worked on this escape—the dirt under his nails is damp and crumbly, and feeling it roll out between his fingers, he remembers how he was nearly caught in the tunnel they dug with spoons and shoes and hands even to get so far as the guard-house—the determination is cool and hard. The third one, the youngest one, with the shocked black hair and the stunned eyes crouches behind the other two. Think of a smooth pool of water. Then think of something bright thrust up from below, a power-blade, its sparks glittering in the surface ripples. This is how the idea of freedom thrusts from his young, arrogant mind.' As Larta spoke, the rain began, thin and gentle through the night.

''Roq said, 'They huddle closer. A cord is tied across the guard-house steps in front of the entrance that faces back towards the shacks. The rear guard always leaves this way a moment before the forward guard leaves by way of the entrance facing the jungle. The first guard will trip on the cord and cry out. The second guard will run back to see what happened, and they will dash across the spot-lit strip into the trees. Mercury and Iron planned it. The flickering Ruby tied one end of the string, and the Sparkling Blade tied the other. They are waiting, alone with their breathing and the thin rain.' We sat still and waited too. Larta returned to her platoon.

"That's primarily the story," Ptorn said. "The actual escape, how they heard the first guard cry out and the second run, how they sped across the strip and got separated among the dark wet trees; or how in the darkness I tracked beside the Secret Ruby, heard him limping over the damp leaves not seven feet away, heard him stop, hesitate, then whisper, 'Hank, Jon, is that you? For the love of . . .' and then I flicked the hilt of my power-blade, and wet leaves shone with sudden green, and he staggered back and screamed, the Ruby of hate confounded in the corners of his eyes; he screamed again, then fell full face on the soft earth. I drew the blade away, flicked the hilt again, and the sparks died, and his body went out. Or how the chubby one screamed, and screamed, and clutched himself to the dripping trunk, his cheek pressed against bark, and screamed. And the mercury vaporized, and the iron flooded him with hot liquid fear. And at last he cried, still clutching the tree, 'Who are you! and show yourself! It's not fair! Oh please, it's not fair . . .' And we circled him, and circled closer. Or, how we carried the bodies back at dawn, in the rain, and left them in the mud outside the shacks—that is really beyond the story, the real story of the escape."

They had almost reached the barracks. "Why . . .?" began Tel. "Why did you say this to me . . ."

Ptorn smiled. "We only brought back two bodies. The third one, the youngest, got detoured into the radiation fields where we couldn't follow him. He should have died. But he didn't. He escaped. Now you said something about knowing an escaped prisoner, and there's only been one escapee in the past sixteen years. Also you know about the telepaths. And besides, your eyes are funny. Did you know that?"

Tel blinked.

"I'm not a telepath," Ptorn said again. "But any forest guard would have told you that story if you had said what you did. We trust each other with information a lot more than you men do. We . . . perceive things a little more clearly."

"But I still don't understand . . ."

"Look. We're going into basic training tomorrow. In six weeks we'll be facing the enemy. Until then, friend, keep out of any more random games. They may not be as random as you think. And keep your mouth shut."

They turned into the barracks.

CHAPTER THREE

THE ISLAND CITY of Toron is laid out in concentric circles. In the centre along colonnaded streets are the Royal Palace and the towering mansions of the wealthy merchants and industrialists. Buildings stare wide windowed at one another, many of the windows composed of layers of stained glass rotated across one another by hidden machinery. Brass or marbled balconies lip the upper stories. Leisurely people dressed in bright colours wander along the streets.

The outer ring is the water-front, the pier, wharves, public buildings and warehouses. Clinging just inside is the section known as the Devil's Pot, a ravelled webbing of narrow streets where furious grey alley cats stalk wharf rats through over-turned garbage. Living here is the vast labouring population of Toron, and the less vast but vicious underworld of the city, many of them in the roving gangs of malis that ranged inward from the island's rim.

Between the inner and outer rings is a section of indistinct apartments, rooming houses, and even occasional private dwellings, for clerks and crafts-men, salesmen and secretaries; doctors, engineers, lawyers and supervisors; those who had worked hard enough and had been lucky enough to rise out of the confusion of the Pot, and those too weak to cling to the centre who had been flung from the whirling hub.

In a two-room apartment in one of these houses, a woman lay on her back, her eyes closed, her mouth opened, her fingers twined in the bed sheets. She was intensely conscious of the City on both sides of her. And she was trying not to scream.

She clamped her jaws and her eyes snapped open like a doll's. On her door was a name-plate that said—black letters on yellow metal—Clea Rahsok. Rahsok was her real name spelled backwards. Once her father, at her suggestion, had called a branch company of refrigeration equipment "Rahsok." She had been twelve when she suggested the spelling to him. Now she used the disguise for herself. Until three years ago she had lived between her father's house and the University. But then she made three discoveries.

Now she lived alone, and did very little but walk, read, figure in her note-book, lie on her back, and try to keep from screaming.

The first thing Clea had discovered was that some-one she loved, loved with an aching passion that made the back of her neck tingle, that made her jaws clench and her stomach suddenly flatten itself whenever she thought of him (his short red hair, his broad taurine body, his sudden grin and the deep inside laughter like a bear's growl)—this someone was dead.

The second thing she had discovered (she had been working on it for half her stay at the University and nine-tenths of the time that she was supposed to be spending on the government project she had joined right after she received her degree) was inverse sub-trigonometric functions and their application to random spacial co-ordinates. The result was a paper presented to the University and then again before a select board of government councillors. The conclusion still threaded through her mind: ". . . and so, gentlemen, it is more than conceivable that by converting the already extant transit-ribbon, we may send between two hundred and three hundred pounds of matter anywhere on the globe with a pinpoint accuracy of microns." Anywhere! Anywhere at all!

The third thing she had discovered—

Something first about her mind. It was a hard, brilliantly honed mathematical mind. Once she, along with fifty other mathematicians and physicists, had been handed three pages of radiation data in order to discover a way over, under, or around it. She had looked at it for three minutes (having put off picking it up for three days while she scribbled in her note-book on her own pet project) and announced that the radiation was artificial, generated by a single projector that could be destroyed, and had thus solved the problem. In short it was a mind that cut through information to the correct answer even when the incorrect question had been asked.

—she had discovered this third thing when she had been assigned to work on a small section of a top secret government project after the presentation of her paper on subtrigonometric functions. She was not told what the project was nor the significance of her part, but her mind, extrapolating from her fragment, had carved and carved at the mystery. It was part of some immensely complex computer, whose purpose, apparently, must be . . . must be . . .!

Her body jerked upright in the bed, the sheets fell from her breasts, and she was breathing very fast in the darkness.

When she made this discovery, she disappeared. Easiest was the trivial disguise of her name. Hardest was convincing her father to let her take this apartment. Between them, the careful destruction of some government records: all copies of her contracts of work for the crystallizing war effort, and the record of her retina pattern on file from her birth. She banked on the general war confusion to keep them from searching her out. After she was established in her two small rooms, she methodically began to dull the edge of that amazing mind.

She went for longer and longer periods away from her books, tried to ignore the war propaganda that flooded the city, made as few decisions as possible, and if she did not succeed in actually blunting it, she sufficiently blurred its keenness to accomplish the same end.

She thought a lot about the person who had died, less about subtrigonometric functions, and when she came anywhere near the third thing, she would think immediately of something else, about not screaming, not screaming, keeping silent and still.

Crumpled on her desk was a poster she had once peeled from a board fence. Across the green paper, scarlet letters proclaimed:

WE HAVE AN ENEMY BEYOND
THE BARRIER

Clea put on her bathrobe, walked to the desk, and reached for the poster. Suddenly she went into the front room without turning on the light. Her clothes were over the back of a chair. In the dark she put them on. Then she went to the door, stepped into the hall, and went to the stairs. Blue-grey dust wedged into the corners.

At the front door she saw Dr. Wental trying to get in. When she opened it for him, he grinned at her, scratched his thin, wrapping-paper hair, and crashed into the doorjamb.

"Dr. Wental!" Clea said. "Are you all right?"

Still smiling, the doctor nodded vigorously. "Spirits . . ." he said. "You be quiet, now. We have to get upstairs quietly so my wife won't . . ." His Adam's apple gave a little leap and he tapped his lips with his fist, guiltily. ". . . won't know. Quietly." His extended arm landed on Clea's shoulder and he sagged against her as his knees gave in different directions. "Beautiful green spirits, Miss Rahsok. If you will excuse a terrible pun, I am in really fine . . ." But he hiccoughed again. "But many too many, much too much. Will you help me upstairs, Miss Rahsok, quietly?"

Clea sighed, and supported Dr. Wental along the hall. "So my wife won't know," he said again. "Oh, this war is a dreadful thing. We have an enemy beyond the barrier, but what it's doing to us back here, in Toromon . . ." He shook his head. "You have to work so hard to get ahead and get the better things in life. But it's hard." He paused to shake his head again. "Occasionally you just have to let go . . ." At the word "go" he slipped back down two of the six steps they had negotiated. Clea whispered "*damn*" and clutched the handrail. "You know," continued Dr. Wental, "all this increased production, of all sorts of equipment? And a good civilian just can't get ahold of any of it. I've got a man coming to me tomorrow with a case of lupus erythermatosis. He was recommended to me by a specialist. I did some research in it a few years ago, and I came up with a few things too. But how can you treat lupus erythermatosis without adrinocorticotropic hormone? You look in the General Medical catalogue and there should be enough around to treat an army—if I can coin a phrase. But try to get it and somebody in a white smock tells you, I'm sorry. Private doctors can only get minimum rations during this period.' What am I going to tell this man. Go away? I can't treat you? I can't get the drug? And he had as much money as the sea has salt. One of the Tildons. I'm an honest man, Miss Rahsok, just trying to get the better things for my family. That's all, really.'' They had reached the doctor's door when the doctor fell against the wall. The forefinger of his left hand pressed against his lips for quiet, while he tried to put his thumb into the print lock.

As Clea went down the hall again, she heard the raspy whisper behind her, ''Quietly, quietly, so my wife won't know.''

Outside, the breeze from the sea lapped the houses and wedged into the streets. Clea's black dress was snapped tight around her neck, and her black hair (once it had been braided with silver chain, and she had danced in a white dress with a man who had short red hair, whose shoulders were box broad, whose words were quietly wise, whose laugh was like a bear's growl, who wore a military uniform . . . and who was dead)—her black hair was tight back in a bun that took her fifteen minutes each morning to brush, comb, and roll up so straight and lacquer stiff.

Carefully, so carefully she unsnapped her collar, and as the flap fell open, she sucked coolness into her chest, deep against her diaphragm. She walked on more easily.

"Hey, lady."

She jumped, but it was an officer. As he approached, his uniform changed from the dull colour of the undersides of oak leaves to olive as he stepped into the ring of light from the street lamp.

"Isn't it sort of late for you to be wandering the streets like this? Malis from over in the Pot beat up a man and near killed him last night just six blocks from here. You'd better go on home."

"Yes sir," Clea said.

The officer walked on, but Clea stood a moment. Then she turned and started away. When she had gone twenty steps, she glanced back, perhaps to see if the officer was watching.

Under the street lamp where she had been a minute before was a girl with white, silken hair. Clea frowned just as the girl dodged to the side—and vanished!

Clea opened her mouth. The moment the girl had stepped out of the direct beam of the lamp, she had disappeared, gone out like a candle flame. Clea blinked. Then she turned and hurried towards home.

Halfway she stopped. About three blocks away, she recalled, was an all night bar with a monumental array of pin-ball-, slot-, and bowling-machines.

She came home at six o'clock the next morning. The bartender for the last two hours had simply leaned on the counter and watched the woman with the tight bun and the high black dress who drank only soft drinks and amassed phenomenal scores on the gaming machines. A woman with a scarf around her head was setting out a garbage can in front of the building.

"Up bright and early, Miss Rahsok?" asked the woman, wiping her hands on her check house dress. "It's good to get up early and take a walk. Shows a proper attitude. With this war on it's so hard to stay cheerful. I just wish we could send letters to our boys, or hear what it was like, or send packages. Then it would be so much easier. Sometimes I just wish I had a son to be proud of . . . But it's still hard on a woman with daughters. Now you take my oldest daughter, Renna. You think she would appreciate how hard it is? What with all the really eligible young men off beyond the barrier a girl has to be particularly careful who she knows, who she goes with. I keep trying to introduce her to nice boys, but she will just pick up with anybody. Oh, it's awful. If a girl's going to get ahead, she's got to be careful. Renna has been seeing some dreadful boy for years named Nonik. Vol Nonik. And do you know where his parents live?" She pointed towards the Pot. "And he doesn't even live with them."

"Excuse me," Clea interrupted. "I . . . I have some work to do and I've got to get upstairs. Excuse me."

"Oh, of course, of course," said the woman, stepping back from the doorway. "But you know a girl can't be too careful."

Inside the apartment, Clea stood by the closed door, thinking, "His arms were strong. He caught me from behind once when we were walking single file along the stone wall by the wharf. His laugh was like a bear's growl; he laughed when we watched the two squirrels chattering at one another on the campus lawn the day he came to visit me at University Island, and his words were quiet and wise. He told me, 'You have to decide what you want.' And I said, 'I want to work on my project with the subtrigonometric functions, and I want to be with you, but if this war—' And suddenly I realised how profound a thing he'd told me then, and realised that having said what I wanted out loud, to him, they were so much easier to have, even though the war . . . the war! He's dead!'' —and stopped thinking.

On the desk she saw her slide-rule and her notebook sticking from under the crumpled poster, and she remembered, ''. . . in brief, what all this mathematical hodge-podge boils down to, gentlemen, is that these inverse subtrigonometric functions do apply to the random spacial co-ordinate system I've outlined and define it prescisely; and so, gentlemen, it is more than conceivable that by converting the already extant transit-ribbon, we may send between two hundred and three hundred pounds of matter anywhere on the globe with a pin-point accuracy of microns.'' Anywhere! Anywhere at all!—and stopped thinking.

She closed the window, lay down on the bed, and again memories flooded her mind. She had begun work on the computer not long after the paper. ''Something for an input that will take information from one and a half to three and a quarter killo-specs, and can handle at least forty thousand data, that's the first thing you can work on.'' Quite idly she assumed that it must be an input that takes information directly from the human brain, seeing as the neo-neanderthal's brain energy had just been measured at one and a half killo-specs while the strange cortex of the brains of the forest guards produced up to three and a quarter. No, it was not an obvious co-relation to make. But she had the information and made the connection as someone else might reason that a thermometer whose specifications stated that it read at least ten degrees higher than ninety-eight point six would be employed taking abnormal human temperatures. Later on she saw on a collegue's desk a schematic for a switchover circuit for the same voltage differential that would change an input to an output. Removing or establishing up to forty thousand bits of information directly into a human mind, she pondered. She solved the problem of the forty thousand data by getting tri-faceted tetron crystals to respond to a frequency-multi-frequency hum and coding the overtones. With ten crystals—each about the size of a pinhead—she achieved a sorting system that would handle sixty-seven thousand, one hundred and forty-nine data (three to the tenth power) and was quite proud of her margin. Once, while exploring the far wing of the building where she worked, she saw through an open door where an artist had left pinned to the wall several sketches of grotesque, imaginary marsh-scapes, and some structurely impossible anatomical dissections. Two weeks later rumour got around that two artists working in the building had undergone prefrontal lobotomy at the insistence of the government psychiatrists. Some other tiny things: a messenger carrying those same sketches and a spool of magnetic tape into an office two flights down; what might have been the same spool changing hands between a white smocked technician and a military official; her own inquiry after the pictures: "Oh those? They were burned. They weren't needed any more," said the violet-eyed lab technician; what seemed like the sudden disbandment of the entire project and she was set to something else; the first reports from the conversion of the transit-ribbon from wire- to wireless-matter transmitter; and then a conversation at lunch with an acquaintance from an entirely different department: ". . . doing work on a weird computer. It puts information right into the brain with tapes. I can't imagine what a human brain is going to do with sixty-seven thousand bits of information, but that's what its output is. Can you imagine?" Clea imagined. One or two other minor details came along. Then one day she was walking by the wharves late one evening when the sky was the hue of split sapphires between the long red clouds, when it hit her: One—he was dead! Two—Anywhere! Anywhere at all! Three—. . . . She stopped thinking. She was going to scream.

Think about something else, about not screaming, about being still, about nothing . . . Slowly the tension eased from her throat, from her fists, from her calves, and she slept.

Late that afternoon she got up, washed her teeth, hands, wrists, neck, and face. She ate. Then she went out to buy the next day's food. Somewhere among all this she had worked out a novel way of calculating every other place of pi, but she had forgotten it by the time she again wandered along the evening streets with darkness rolling towards her.

The first sound that jerked her mind to the surface was a cry to her left. There were footsteps in the alley beside her, a thud, another cry, then several sets of footsteps. At first she started to turn away, but something made her go forward.

She looked around the corner, then pressed back

against the wall. Malis! Two men and then a woman ran forward to where an already indistinguishable number of people were brawling in the street. Someone jumped back, a man was kicked hard in the stomach and rolled over the pavement. A woman screamed, cursed, and staggered with hands over her eyes.

Someone broke loose from the fray, a girl—with white hair!

Clea felt something catch in her gut. The girl ran in a diagonal taking her vaguely in Clea's direction. Then two men were suddenly in front of her. Something fanned white sparks as one man raised his arms.

A power-blade!

As the arm descended, Clea saw the reflection near her feet, a thin white line against a disc of water. She reached down, grabbed the bucket from beneath the drainpipe at her side and dashed the contents over the figures. The power-blade shorted, steamed, and went out, falling harmlessly across the white-haired girl's arm.

But now her safe position behind the drain was known. The girl, dancing back, looked at Clea, and Clea looked back. Her eyes! she thought. Good Lord, she has no eyes!

But someone was coming towards her, now: the man with the power-blade. His grin looked like the split rind of a rotten kharba fruit. She kicked at him and dodged, thinking (the way she would think of the fluxuation in the second derivative of a fourth degree log function, sharply, coolly) he supports his weight mostly on his left foot and uses his right to propel himself, and when she was about to be overtaken, she whirled to face him and brought the side of her shoe down hard on the top of his right foot—he was barefooted—at the same time jamming her elbow in the darkness that was his stomach.

As he went down under her double attack, she fled, hearing her own footsteps, then others in counterpoint, lighter, overtaking hers. Again she whirled, thinking, I will throw myself at whoever it is and bite for the neck; they won't expect that.

But she stopped when she turned, the thought ludicrously rising in her mind like a thin blade from beneath a smooth surface: but she does have eyes, bright blue eyes!

They were under street lamp.

"Come on," the white-haired girl said. "Down this way. They're still coming!"

They turned the next corner, ran the block, dodged down two more alleys, then slowed.

Clea jerked the air into her lungs, trying to form the words, *All right, who are you?* her tongue working over them as over an anticipated taste when the girl said:

"Hey, you fight good."

Surprised, Clea looked at the girl and said instead, "Thank you." Then she said. "Your arm! What's wrong with your arm?"

Huh?" She was holding her left hand across her right shoulder. "Oh, nothing."

"You're hurt," Clea said. She looked up at the sign. "Look, I live eight blocks from here. Come on up and I'll put something on it," and find out who you are, she remembered to add, silently.

"Sure, Dr. Koshar," the girl said. "Thanks."

Clea jumped, or something inside her did, but she started walking.

In front of her door, her finger poised before the

print lock, Clea asked, "Who sent you after me? And call me by my first name."

"All right," the girl said.

The door swung in and Clea turned on the light. "What's your name?"

"Alter," said the girl.

"Sit down over there, Alter, and take your blouse off."

Clea went into the bathroom and returned with three small bottles, a roll of tape, and one of gauze. "You haven't told me who sent you yet. Ehhh . . . That looks as if someone took a vegetable grater to your shoulder."

"I guess you shorted the blade, but it was still a little hot. My arm was hurt badly once before and I'm always a little wary." She added, "You haven't let me tell you yet."

"I wonder where they get those weapons anyway. Only the guards and the military are supposed to have them."

"From the guards and the military," Alter said. She winced as transparent liquid flowed across the raw skin and relaxed as red liquid followed it. "Nobody sent me here, really."

"Maybe I don't want to know." Suddenly the brittle tone she was trying to maintain broke and warmth flooded from beneath. "What's this?" she asked, fingering a loop of leather thongs from the girl's neck on which were strung polished shells of green, red, and golden browns.

"A boy gave it to me," Alter said. "It's just a necklace."

"It's been broken once," Clea said. "But it's been fixed."

"That's right. So was my arm," Alter said. "How did you know?"

"Because there're cuts in the surface of the leather around the shells on the right hand side, as if something heavy came down on it and crunched the pieces on that side against the leather. And your shoulder's slightly enlarged. But I'm sure it works well."

Alter looked up, her wide eyes like turquoises behind her tanned face. "That's right, someone stepped on it . . . once." Then she asked, "Why did you tell me that?"

"Because I'm astute. And I want you to know it." Criss-cross, criss-cross, four strips of tape went over the gauze padding on Alter's shoulder. Clea went to the freezer, took out some fresh fruit, and brought it to the table. "You hungry?"

"Um-hm," Alter said, and fell on the fruit, looking up once to say a full *Thank you*. When she was about half finished, Clea said, "You see if the government sent you, there's no reason for my even trying to get away. But if somebody else did, then . . ."

"Your brother," Alter said. "And Arkor, and the Duchess Petra."

"What about my brother," Clea said softly.

"He didn't send me," said Alter, biting into the fruit, "exactly. But they told me where you were, and so I decided to come and see what kind of person you were."

"What kind of person am I?"

"You fight good," Alter grinned.

Clea smiled back. "How's Jon?"

"Fine," said Alter. "All in one piece."

"In three years I heard from him only twice. Did he have a message?"

Alter shook her head.

"Well, I'm glad he's alive," said Clea, moving the bottles together on the table.

"What they're trying to do with the war—"

"I don't want to hear about it." Clea stood up, and took the bottles back in the bathroom. "I don't want to hear anything about the damned war." When she closed the medicine chest, she looked in the mirror for the length of a held breath.

When she came out, Alter had gone to the desk, pushed aside the crumpled poster, and was looking through the notebook. "What's all this?"

Clea shrugged.

"You invented the thing that sends you over the barrier, didn't you?" Alter asked after a moment.

Clea nodded.

"Is that what this is about?"

"That's just fooling around."

"Can you explain how the barrier thing works?"

"It would take me all night, Alter. And you wouldn't understand it anyway."

"Oh," Alter said. "I can't stay up all night because I have to see about a job tomorrow."

"Oh?" asked Clea. "Then I guess you can sleep here. What were those malis after you for?"

"I was out," Alter said. "And so were they. That's how they work."

Clea frowned. "And you don't have anywhere else to stay?"

"There was a place I thought I could sleep at, an inn over in the Pot, but it's been torn down. So I was just wandering around, I've been away for a while."

"Away where?"

"Just away." Then she laughed. "You tell me about how that over the barrier thing works, and I'll tell you about where I was. Your brother was there."

"It's a deal," Clea said. "But in the morning."

Alter went over to the sofa and lay down with her

face to the back so that her bandaged shoulder was up. Clea went to her bed. Before she sat down, without turning, she said, "I thought I saw you following me last night."

"That's right," came the voice from the sofa.

"And suddenly you disappeared."

"That's right."

"Explain."

"Ever head of viva-foam?"

"No."

"Neither had I until four days ago. And until this morning I never had my hands on any. It's a plastic pigmented spray with pores. I'm covered with it. Otherwise, in dim light you couldn't see me."

"You'll have to go into that in more detail tomorrow."

"Sure."

Clea sat down on the bed. "Those malis were just out? Where do they come from? What do they want . . . ?"

"Aren't you sort of a mali too?" Alter asked after a moment.

"How do you mean?"

"A malcontent," Alter said. "Why are you holed up here, hiding from everybody like this? With some people it turns inward, with others it turns out, I guess."

"You know everything, don't you." She chuckled.

The sound of a yawn came from the sofa.

What am I doing here? Clea wondered, and thought about that, instead of screaming.

Early morning slapped red-gold across the wall. Someone was in the bathroom. Water splashed against the porcelain washbowl.

Then Alter walked out. "Hi," she grinned.

"Where are you off to?"

"The circus," Alter said. "To get a job. Want to go with me?"

Clea frowned.

"Come on," Alter said. "Getting out will do you good."

Clea stood up, went into the bathroom, washed her face, and came out coiling the hank of black hair laboriously into a tight, black bun.

"Braid it," Alter said from behind her.

"What?"

"Why don't you braid it. It'll take half the time and it won't look so . . ." She gave a nameless little shudder.

Clea let her hair fall to her shoulders again, then reached up and divided it into three.

When they came out in the street, Clea's collar was open and her hair hung in a thick black braid over her shoulder.

Only a few people were out. The sun set crowns of light on the towers of the City. Gold caught on a balcony railing, snagged on a bright window as the sun descended to street level.

"Which direction?" Clea asked, pausing to look at the towers.

"This way."

They walked between the buildings towards the Devil's Pot.

In that crushed together rim of the City a vacant lot was a rare thing. The Triton Extravaganza ("The Greatest Spectacle of Entertainment on Island, Sea, or Continent") had commandeered a two block area and set up its emporium. Criss-cross ropes webbed green and purple canvas against the sky. Cage upon cage lined one side of the lot: pumas, an eight-legged bison, a brown bear, a two-headed fox, a giant boar; and a five thousand-gallon aquarium housed a quivering albino squid. In another, tiger sharks nosed the glass corners, while further on an octopus ravelled and unravelled over blue sand.

A covey of bright aerial artists ran from one tent, broke about them, and disappeared into another. "Who . . . ?" Clea began.

"Trapeze workers," Alter said. "They call themselves the Flying Fish. Corny. Come on; I've got to see Mr. Triton."

"What's over there?" Clea asked as they started towards the large wagon at the end of the lot with its great papier maché neptune bearded, big bellied, and beaming from the roof.

Huh? That's the chow wagon. Hey, why don't you go over there and get something to eat while I see Mr. Triton? I'll join you later but I have to audition on an empty stomach, or there'll be hell to pay."

"Well, I . . ." But Alter was up the steps of the big wagon; and Clea was alone. The morning was noisy and cool.

She turned towards the cook-tent where a green and yellow awning overhung wooden tables. Grease sizzled on the grill. Clea sat down across from a man sipping chowder from a terracotta mug. He gave her a grin that pulled the sudden net of wrinkles tight around his smokey eyes.

A waitress at her shoulder said, "What'll it be, come on now. I don't got all day, please?"

"What do you have?"

The waitress frowned. "Fried fish, boiled fish, broiled fish, fish roe, fish and chips—special is eggs and fried fish, fifty centi-units."

"The special," Clea said.

"Fine," the waitress smiled. "Surprise! It's edible today."

The man across the table grinned again and asked, "What sort of act do you do?"

Just then a woman in a spangled jumper sat down beside the man and said, "Is she one of the new auditions?"

"I'm a clown," the man volunteered.

"Oh . . . I . . . a . . . don't have an act."

Both the man and the woman laughed.

"I mean I don't have an act in the circus."

They laughed again and the woman nodded. "I just train seals, honey, so don't hassle."

Just then the waitress slipped a plate of fillet and scrambled eggs, with butter streaming through the yellow hills, down to the white crock plate. Clea picked up the fork, and the clown said, "Honey, you enjoy eating don't you?"

Surprised, Clea looked at him, and then down at herself.

"No, I don't mean your weight. I mean the way you look at food. Someone who looks at food like that, like it was the very special experience it is, that sort of person never has to worry about their figure." He turned to the seal trainer. "You know what I mean? With their look, you know why they're fat as a tug. Or if their eyes get slightly narrow and their mouths purse in, then you've got the reason why they're as thin as rails. But the look you gave—" he said, turning back to Clea.

"Oh, shut up," the seal trainer said. "You start talking and we'll be here all day." Clea and the two circus folk laughed. Then the clown said, "Hey," and was looking over Clea's shoulder and far behind.

She turned.

Across the lot someone had set up a trampoline. In

regular bounds the white-haired girl vaulted and spun against the sky: back triple somersault, front triple somersault, half gainer, recovery, full gainer, recovery, jackknife opening backwards in a reverse swan, triple back, then triple front again . . .

"She's good!" the clown said.

The seal trainer nodded.

Triple forward, triple forward, swan, triple back. Then straight candle through a quadruple back into a full gainer, closing with a double forward before she hit the elastic for the last time.

People over the entire lot had stopped to look. Now roustabouts, sidewalls, and performers set up a scattering of applause.

Alter was coming towards the cook tent. Beside her a man had his arm around her shoulder. He was elderly, rotund, and a great cotton-ball beard fluffed across his chest.

Clea rose to make room for them at the table, then glanced around and saw to her surprise that everybody else at the table was standing too. There was a sudden, uneven, but cheerful chorus of, "Hello, Mr. Triton. Good morning, Mr. Triton."

"Sit down, sit down," proclaimed Triton expansively, and chairs slid back into place. Now he continued talking to Alter. "So you'll join us the day after tomorrow. Very fine. Very fine. Do you have a place to stay, because you're perfectly welcome to sleep on the lot."

"Thank you," Alter said. "Oh, this is my friend I was telling you about."

Surprise pulled down the corners of Clea's mouth before she caught them back up in a defensive smile.

"You're an accountant, right? Well, I could use somebody to get the books in order. We'll be doing quite a business on the mainland tour. Be here with the kid—''

''But I . . .'' Clea began, looking to Alter who was grinning again.

''—the day after tomorrow,'' finished Mr. Triton, ''and the job's yours. Good morning, everybody. Good morning.'' Then he paused, looked hard at Clea, and said, ''You know, I like the way you look. I mean the way you look *at* things.'' Then he called again, ''Good morning.''

''What did I tell you,'' said the clown to the seal trainer.

''But I . . .'' Clea repeated. Mr. Triton was walking away. '' . . .I don't want a job—I don't think . . .''

Alter was shaking hands with the seal trainer, the clown, and even the waitress who was congratulating her. A moment later she looked around to say something to Clea; but Clea was gone.

She walked, looking neither at the smoky faces of the clapboard buildings on her left, nor the screaming boy hurling chunks of pavement at a three-legged dog to her right. She looked neither at the littered gutters nor at the pale towers that rose in the centre of the City. She walked straight ahead until she reached her apartment building.

''Oh, Miss Rahsok, there you are. Out early as usual.'' It was not yet eight-thirty.

''Oh . . . hello.''

''Like I always say,'' said the woman, adjusting her head scarf, ''it's always good to get out bright and early.'' Suddenly the expression on the woman's face reversed itself, and she repeated. ''Speaking of bright and early, do you know what my daughter Renna . . . well, she sneaked out of here at sunrise this morning, and I know she's run off to spend the day with that Vol Nonik character. We were arguing about him last night. What are his prospects? I asked her. After all, I'm a reasonable woman. What does he intend to do with himself? And do you know what she told me? He writes poems! And that's all! Well, I had to laugh. But I have a surprise for her that I'm sure will drive this Nonik individual out of her head. I got an invitation for her to the Victory League Ball. I had to wrangle with Mrs. Mulqueen half an hour. But if Renna goes she'll meet some nice young man and forget this idiot boy and his idiot poems. Why isn't a young man like Nonik off in the army? We have an enemy beyond the barrier, and I ask you . . .''

"Excuse me," Clea said. "Excuse me, please."

"Oh, of course. I didn't mean to keep you. Good morning.

But Clea had already pushed past and was walking up the stairs. We have an enemy beyond the barrier. She thought of the poster crumpled on her desk, and like the stimulus of a conditioned reflex, it released:

His arms strong, confident around me as his laughter and wisdom were confident, his bright eyes blinking in sudden sunlight, and the bear growl tenderness—he's dead;

". . . we may send between two hundred and three hundred pounds of matter anywhere on the globe with a pin-point accuracy . . ." Anywhere at all;

That computer, what else could they use it for, that insanely programmed, crazy, random . . .

Then she had slammed the door behind her, razoring the scream building in her throat. She leaned against the door, tasting the breaths that plunged again and again into her lungs so hard they hurt.

She did not go out again all day. It was not until

midnight that she managed to make herself leave the room for a walk. But as she reached the stairs, she heard a crash. Someone had just fallen at the foot.

Frowning, she hurried down the steps. The someone uncrumpled, grinned at her, and put a finger to his lips. "Shhhh. Please, shhhh. So my wife won't know!"

"Are you all right?"

"Of course I'm all right." Then his Adam's apple lunged upward. "Oh, excuse me. I'm perfectly all right. Really in very fine . . ."

"So I gather. Just a moment. Here you go, Dr. Wental."

They started up the stairs, the doctor chuckling. "Oh, the trials and tribulations that a man must go through. Oh, the trials." He gave another burp. "Got that poor old lupus erythermatosis case in this afternoon. Did I say poor? Excuse me. I meant 'bloody rich'. In a month he'll be swollen as a blow-fish. But what can you do when General Medical won't give out an adrinocorticotropic hormone? Gave him a shot of good old saline solution with a bit of food colouring. It certainly won't hurt him and I charged him fifty units. He'll be back tomorrow. Maybe I'll be able to get some by then. But it's terribly hard, Miss Rahsok. I could almost cry."

As they reached the door, Dr. Wental motioned for silence a final time. She left him fumbling for the print lock. When she reached the front door, she stopped.

This time she did not think of her three discoveries. She thought instead, very briefly, about Renna's mother, Renna, and Vol Nonik. She knew the name from somewhere—then she thought about Dr. Wental, Dr. Wental's patient, and Dr. Wental's wife. Outside night pressed against the glass door, but beyond she could just hear the last faint tinkle of the calliope from the circus blocks away. She came back up to her room early.

The next morning, her hair in a braid, her collar opened back from her throat, she walked along the street toward the circus lot. Morning chill cooled the shadowed half of her face while the sun stroked the other with yellow fingers. The sea smell came strong from the wharves, and she was smiling.

As she walked by the fence that rimmed the already bustling lot, she saw someone coming toward her. A flash of silver hair, and Alter, laughing, ran toward her and caught her hand. "Gee, I'm glad you came back!"

"Why shouldn't I?" Clea said. "Though it was touch and go for a while. Why didn't you come back to my place? You could have stayed there. You had me worried."

Alter looked down. "Oh," she said. "I thought you might be angry. It was sort of a funny thing to pull." With one hand Alter was fumbling with her necklace.

"What possessed you to tell Mr. Triton I wanted a job?"

"It just hit me that it might be fun. And maybe you would get a kick out of it."

"Well thanks. Hey, I hope your friend who gave you that comes around some day. Did he put them logarithmically increasing distances on purpose?"

"Huh?" asked Alter. "No, I don't think so. He's off in the war now . . . Hey, did I say something?"

"The war? No— He can't . . ."

"What is it?"

"Nothing," Clea said. Suddenly she put her arm around Alter's shoulder and gave her a friendly squeeze.

"Are you sure you're all right?"

Clea took a breath and let her arm fall away. "I'm sure," she said.

They walked together into the lot.

CHAPTER FOUR

THE NEXT DAY Tel began basic training:

"All right, you guys. Split up into your respective groups and report to your instruction rooms."

He came into a large classroom the far wall of which was covered with charts of machinery. There were no labels on the charts. Across the front wall stretched a full colour swamp-scape, wreathed in mist and spiked with serpentine, leafless vegetation. A loudspeaker in the front of the room suddenly announced in a friendly voice (friendly, though oddly ambiguous as to sex, he noticed): "Take your seats everyone. We are beginning your basic training."

The recruits shuffled to their places at the metal desks.

"You are in the wrong seat, Private Rogers," said the loudspeaker affably. "Two to your left."

A baffled blond boy looked up, then dutifully moved two seats over.

"I am going to read a list of names out loud," continued the speaker. "Everyone whose name I call must leave here and report to room 46-A. That is two flights up and along the corridor to your right. Now: Malcon 831 BQ-N, Motlon 601 R-F, Orley 015 CT-F . . ." Everyone looked a little puzzled, but the named recruits rose and went out of the room.

When nearly half the room was emptied, the loudspeaker said: "Now, those of you who are left take your earphones and put them on. Now look into your vision-hoods."

Tel slipped his earphones over his ears and rested his forehead on the support above the masked hood on the table. The magnified screen before him flickered with merging light, misty and indistinct, mostly blues and greens, faint red blushes here and there, a tide drifting slowly, too slowly.

Windy music came through the phones. Then a gruff but pleasant masculine voice began: "We have an enemy beyond the barrier. We have been able to reach past the radiation barrier only a few years, but already we have discovered a menace of such inhuman and malignant design . . ."

The voice droned and the colours coalesced, forming at last a recognizable beach. Sand arched away to the horizon, blue waves broke into white froth that scudded over the beach. A girl with a remarkable figure, wearing a skimpy bathing suit, came to the water's edge, touched her toe to the foam, then turned, seemed to see him, and began to run, laughing, towards him. The breeze tossed her auburn hair. Her lips parted and he could hear waves.

Dr-r-r-r-r-r-r—!

Tel jumped back from the masked screen, slamming his spine into the back of the chair. He tore the earphones from his head. The relief as they clattered to the desk was as if two needles of pure sound had been ripped from his ears. His eyes still flickered with the after image of a blinding white light that had suddenly flooded the screen. Around him the room was in confusion, and somewhere a woman was laughing.

The laugh articulated itself, became a voice. "All right. All right. Resume your seats in an orderly manner. Resume your seats," Many of the soldiers had leapt from their chairs.

The feminine voice continued over the loudspeaker. "Your reaction to that last problem was not what we hope it will be at the end of your six week course. You men who just came in—" Tel now realized that a group of completely bewildered recruits had just come in and were standing by the door. "—did they look to you like anyone ready to fight the enemy beyond the barrier?"

Tel felt confused and uncomfortable.

"All during your basic training," continued the lilting alto, "you will be presented with problems of this nature. We want calmness, alertness, and quick reactions; not confusion and disorder. Now sometimes the problems may not be as obvious as that, but watch for them. Remember, we want calmness, alertness, and quick reactions. Will you recruits who have just arrived please take your seats. Everyone reguard your screens and place your headphones on."

Tel noted as he bent forward that the half of the class who had been in the room the whole period were a lot slower in putting on their earphones than the newcomers.

On the magnified screen an explanation was in progress concerning a piece of equipment called 606-B. He was shown in detail how to take it apart, put it together, and keep its numerous parts, mechanical and electronic, in smooth order. But somehow (perhaps he missed it during the twenty seconds at the beginning when he'd hesitated over the earphones) no matter how hard he concentrated, he hadn't the faintest idea what 606-B was used for. But by the time the film had continued for forty minutes, he was sure he could have put one of the damn things together in his sleep.

A gentle bell signalled the end of the period, and everyone raised his head. Tel checked his programme card for his next room and got up to go. Apparently all the newcomers were assigned to stay in the same room.

"Hey," someone whispered, and Tel turned at the door. In the corner seat among the remaining recruits sat Shrimp. Tel nodded to him, but Shrimp looked perplexed. "Hey," he whispered again. So Tel went over to him. "What the hell did they do to you when we came in? You guys looked like . . ."

"No talking back there!" The voice from the loudspeaker this time was definitely masculine. "You in the back there, get a move on! Proceed quietly and quickly to your next class."

Tel left the room.

Two flights up he entered a room nearly identical to the one he'd left. Again the walls were covered with charts of nameless machines. The marsh-scape spread across the front of the room. He was looking for the 606-B when a fatherly, middle-aged voice announced from the loudspeaker: "Everyone sit down. I am going to read a list of names out loud. All those I call will please report to room 51-D. Now, Ritter 67 N-T, Ptorn 047 AA-F, Tynan 811 NA-T . . ."

Tel hadn't even realized Ptorn was in the same room with him.

After lights-out they talked for a while in the dark:

Shrimp: "Hey, Lug, What did you learn today?"

Lug (grunting from the bunk beneath): "To put it together, take it apart, keep the central shaft vertical . . . Aw, go to sleep."

Tel: "Hey, was that the 606-B?"

Lug: "Seven thirty something or other. Go to sleep. I'm tired."

Shrimp (calling upward to Ptorn): "What did you big boys learn about today?"

Ptorn: "Not enough to talk about now. We've got to be up at six tomorrow. We have an enemy beyond the barrier, remember?"

Shrimp: "Yeah, I remember. G'night."

Ptorn: "Night."

Tel: "Hey Lug, what's the seven thirty something used for, huh?"

Lug: (A yawn from the lower birth; then snoring.)

There is the gentle sound of breathing. Someone coughs. Someone turns over and the snoring stops. Then silence as Tel's ears filled with sleep.

The next week the platoon was shown a documentary film. The men filed into the auditorium and took their seats. A few put their knees up against the back of the chair in front of them, other puffed on the plankton cigarettes they had been issued. Tel had never found their taste particularly pleasant. They contained some mildly tranquilizing drug that only made him dizzy. The lights darkened, the screen flickered, and without titles the movie began.

The opening shot Tel recognized as a foggy

swamp-scape similar to the ones at the head of so many of the classrooms. Green mud sucked and bubbled around the stalks of twining plants. Mist scarfed over the silt and writhed about the tines. The scene shifted to a more solid stretch of land, passed by a boulder, a depression in the ground, a fragment of machinery (was it the 606-B? The camera moved too quickly for him to be certain), at last stopped in front of the ruins of an army barracks. One of the walls was burned away and the roof sagged. The camera dollied through the charred opening into the hut.

A man sits in a chair. His intestines fall over the arm. He has no head. Several bunk beds are over-turned in the corner. On a crumpled pile of bedding is a pile of, approximately, two corpses. The camera dollies out of the shack. Propped against the outside wall, his legs at insane angles, is a grinning soldier. His eyes are dark holes. An insect scurries over his lip and down his chin.

The camera moves on past a wall composed of burlap gravel sacks. Through the thickening mist Tel could make out barbed wire strung across the wall. Fog closes across the camera lens. Then the scene cut.

Through the haze Tel could see a row of huts similar to the gutted one in the previous scene. A few men were walking around.

Close-up shot of a young soldier in need of a shave. He smiles at the camera, blinks, and rubs his chin with greasy fingers. Full shot of the same soldier. He is standing beside a complicated-looking machine (that certainly wasn't the 606-B, Tel thought, Or was it?). He scratches his chest, looks embarrassed, then goes back to fixing the machine.

Cut to shot of barracks building. A group of men have spread boards over the muddy ground. They squat or sit crosslegged on the boards in an irregular circle. Close-up shot of the centre of the circle: someone is setting up a square of fifteen centi-unit pieces with the corner missing. (There is relieved laughter through the auditorium. "Two and six," someone calls out. Tel laughs too.) At some signal which the audience cannot hear, the men look up from their game. Someone scrapes the coins into his palm, and they run off. Shot of the men running across the clearing before the shacks. Shots of men climbing into squat, caterpillar-tread tanks. Shots of tank's plastic observation bubble as driver takes his seat inside. Shot of four tanks starting one after another. Shot of tanks rolling away through the mist, which closes behind them.

Around the twining plants the green mud bubbles. The barracks' shacks are empty. The clearing is deserted.

Cut to:

A tank has stopped in the middle of a thickly overgrown section of swamp, one corner sunk in the mud. Twenty feet away another tank is lying on its side. The camera approaches the first tank. The observation dome has been smashed. One metal side-plate has been twisted away like foil. The camera dollies towards the rent to peer inside the gutted interior where torn and broken . . .

The screen flickered. The lights went on. They had seen nothing through the black gash, but Tel found when he released the armrests of the auditorium chair that his palms were wet. The seat of his pants and backs of his thighs were soaking.

"All right," came the loudspeaker's voice, "report

to your assigned work-shops.''

Ten minutes later Tel was dismantling a machine very like the one the young soldier had been fixing in the film. He removed an oily plate, wiped it on his apron, and looked at it in the bluish light from the work lights on the ceiling. In the right-hand corner neatly inscribed was: 605-B.

He looked at the machine, then he looked up, coughed, and said, ''Eh . . . I think there's been a mistake.'' He felt uncomfortable addressing the thin air. When others asked, they received answers less than half the time.

But the loudspeaker clicked and a man's voice asked, ''What is it, Private Tel 211 BQ-T?''

''Wasn't I supposed to be working on a 606?''

There was a long silence. Then a woman's contralto said, ''The correction will be made when and if necessary.''

Suddenly he felt confusion as a dozen ideas that he was trying to set straight all knotted together like snarled fishing lines. The confusion became rage which immediately retracted into fear. What were they trying to do to him? What was the damn machine used for anyway? And if he didn't know, how could he fight the enemy beyond the . . .

Dr-r-r-r-r-r-r-r. . . !

They flung their hands over their eyes at the blinding flash that came from the blue fixtures. Before the buzzing stopped the words had leapt into his mind so clearly that at first he thought they came from the speakers: calmness, alertness, quick reaction. He froze, beating back the questions that tried to squirm up into his mind.

Slowly he relaxed. He was calm. He was alert. Two or three people in the shop had already gone back to work, so he picked up a connective bar from the parts rack on the table. For one sudden moment he wanted to heave it at something. Instead he fitted it carefully between the busser plates and twisted the helical pin into place.

That evening some of them went out on the rampway and set up a game of randy.

Shrimp: "O.K. big boy, I'll take my chances with you.

Come on, hunker down here, and play me a round."

Ptorn: (shaking his head): "I'm just watching."

Shrimp: "Say, how come you big guys have all been so quiet for the last couple of days? What gives up there in your superior noggins?"

Ptorn: "I'll just watch."

Waggon: "Come on. I got money to lose."

Curly: "Play him, Shrimp. The ape's gotten better. Won fifteen units off me yesterday—before I won back twenty."

Tel: "Hey, Ptorn, why have you guys been so quiet?"

Ptorn (shrugging): "I don't know." (He pauses) "What do you think the enemy beyond the barrier looks like?"

Lug (leaning against the railing, now looks up and scratches his head): "You know, I never thought of that before."

Tel watches the guard and the neanderthal looking across the railing over the City. Far away the meaningless lights blink in their random pattern.

The third week they put him in a dark room. "What's your name and number?"

"Tel 211 BQ-T."

Dr-r-r-r-r-r-r . . .!

He staggered back and covered his eyes. But there had been no flash, he realized a moment later. Calmness, alertness, quick reaction.

"Turn around."

He turned.

"Walk forward."

He walked. He walked a long time, figuring at last that he must have entered a tunnel . . .

Dr-r-r-r-r-r-r . . .!

Calmness, alertness, quick reaction; he kept walking, though the tension in his back and shoulders almost made them hurt. And there had been a flash, this time. But it was green and not that bright. He had glimpsed mist, and sharp plants without leaves, and mud was bubbling someplace . . . No. That was in the front of the room where he had his classes. Or was it someplace else, with the strange machine . . .

"What is your name and number?"

"Eh . . .Tel 211 B . . . eh . . .BQ-T."

"Describe what you see."

"Eh . . . where . . ."

"Describe what you see in front of you. Keep walking."

There was another green flash. "I think . . . the sea?" He said. "Yes, the sea, and there are waves breaking over the sand, and the little boat . . ."

Dr-r-r-r-r-r-r. . . !

"Describe what you see." The light flashed again.

"No. I mean the 605-B, or maybe the 606-B, I'm not sure . . . I have to put it together. I can put both of them together . . . that's right . . . either one. They're almost the same, but they're different down in the drive box. I fix them so . . ." And a sudden thought welled warm and comfortable into his mind, and with it amazing relief that started in his shoulders and washed down to his feet ". . . so we can fight the enemy beyond the barrier. That's what it's for. It must be. It's the 606-B, and I can take it apart and put it together, take it apart and put it . . ."

There was another green light.

"There, yes, the mud, and the plants that haven't any leaves on them, all the mud, and it's foggy. And those are pebbles over there. No, they aren't pebbles. No, they're shells, very pretty, red and brown and milky shells, like somebody polished them for a long—"

D-r-r-r-r-r-r-r-r!

　"—for a long—"

　　Dr-r-r-r-r-r-r-r-r!

　　"—a long—"

　　　D-r-r-r-r-r-r-r-r-r-r!

　　　. . ."—pebbles . . ."

The pain that built in his back, his thighs, his arms, nearly made him collapse before he knew it was there. He stopped talking, staggered back, and put his hands over his eyes, though again there had been no flash.

"What is your name and number."

"Eh . . . Te . . . my number is Tel 60 . . . 5 . . . 6 . . . Tel . . ."

Something gripping at the back of his tongue suddenly released and a scream let loose that had been lodged somewhere in his stomach, "606-B! . . . 605-B! . . . I don't know! I don't know! They wouldn't tell me which one . . .! They wouldn't tell me!"

"What is your name and number."

"Eh . . . eh . . . Tel 211 BQ-T"

"Describe what you see."

"I see . . . I see the mud, and the plants, and the shacks where the soldiers are. They are sitting in front of the shacks, playing randy. I have to fix it while they play with the coins because . . .the enemy . . . yes, the . . ." and beyond the mist, something moved across the mud, something was knocking aside the plants; at first he thought it might be one of the tanks returning, only it wasn't . . . No! "No!" he cried, "it isn't fixed yet! The 606-B, I haven't fixed it yet, and it's coming. Oh Lord, it's . . ."

Dr-r-r-r-r-r-r-r!

Afterwards, when they took him out of the room, the loudspeaker told him (a soothing female voice), "You did well. Very well indeed. You will be an asset against our enemy beyond the barrier." Already he wasn't sure what had happened in the room. But he had done well, and that made him feel good.

That evening, however, the apes played a ran-domax among themselves. Everyone else sat on their bunks and watched the clumsy games of the neanderthals, speaking very little.

CHAPTER FIVE

JON KOSHAR WALKED down one of the radial streets of Toron, past the merchants' mansions, past the hive-houses, into the sprawling rim of the Devil's Pot, past the lot where the Triton Extravaganza was folding its tents to begin its mainland tour, past the wharves where the Shuttle Boat was pulling in with its load of workers from the Hydroponics Gardens. A breeze caught in his black hair; his black eyes were calm as he moved through the surge of men and women erupting from the launch pier. Further down were the private yachts. He walked to the royal pier. The sun across the water snagged in the polished chains. The double mollusc shell, insignia of the Duchess Petra dipped and dofted in the water. A long shadow fell across the dock as Arkor appeared at the rail.

"Hi," Jon called. "What's the news from the University?"

He stepped over the chain and walked to the end of the gang-plank.

"I've spoken to Catham," Arkor said, coming

down to meet him. "He was a bit surprised to see me, I think. You give me the news here and I'll give you mine."

"Apparently Alter is with my sister, so the Duchess reports. And Tel finally went into the army, off to fight the enemy beyond the barrier."

"Catham simply says to find the *Lord of the Flames* and to expel him as fast as possible. Then ask questions."

"Why?"

"He says it's historical necessity. If Chargill hadn't been assassinated already, we could conceivably spend more time figuring this thing out."

"Sounds reasonable."

They left the pier and started up the waterfront street.

After a few minutes of silence, Jon asked, "Arkor?"

"Yes?"

"What do you hear?"

"With my mind?"

"Yes."

"In you?"

"Around me, and in me too."

Arkor smiled. "You must think that's very important, you who can't see what I see, hear what I hear. It isn't though." He paused. "I can sense—that's a better word than hear—about a block in every direction, at least clearly." They rounded a corner. "There's a worker who's remembering how her brother died eating poisoned fish. In that building over there a neanderthal named Jeof who runs a mali gang is having a nightmare about someone he beat up a few nights ago . . . there, now he's dreaming about food and has turned over and closed his teeth on the pillow. Over there a man named Vol Nonik is sitting at a wobbly table in the corner room of the top floor. The late sun through the window strikes his bare chest. He's trying to write a poem about a girl and runs his fingers over the paper. He glances at a sketch of him the girl drew in red chalk and hung on the wall behind him, then writes: *Renna, her brown eyes opening on ocean light . . .* Somewhere in the circus lot I sense a woman with a mind like steel going swiftly through the account books of the Triton Extravaganza . . ." Suddenly he smiled. "It's your sister, Jon." As suddenly a frown replaced it. "Something's wrong."

"What is it," Jon asked, "is she all right?"

"Yes, but it's something . . . in her mind. It's down very deep." Arkor's frown increased. Then he shook his head. "No, I can't sense it. It's almost as if she's hiding it behind something else. I can see the pattern, hear the sound of it, but it's too deep to sense the meaning."

"What do you sense in my mind?" Jon asked when they had gone a few steps farther.

"A cry," said Arkor, "sharp as a blade thrust up from a pool of dark waters."

"A cry for what?"

"For . . . a recognition; a recognition of what you call freedom."

Jon smiled. "I'm glad it's still there. You know, Arkor, I'm committed to do as much as possible to end this war. But I didn't exactly choose to become an agent of the Triple Being. It was a choice of dying in the radiation fields after my escape, or joining them. That's no choice, and I won't be free until they leave us."

"Another thing I hear both in your mind and your

voice is how much you want me to believe you . . ."

"But it's the truth. Go ahead, read my mind . . ."

"I already have," Arkor said. "I wish you could understand this, Jon. You think the main difference between you and me is that I know what you're thinking while you don't know what I think. That's not it. It's far more a difference in perception that exists between all you men and all us guards. The difference between men and the forest guards is the difference between blind men and men who can see. The difference between the guards who can read minds and the guards who can't is the difference between normal and colour-blind vision."

"Which is to say. . . ?"

Arkor sighed. "Which means that what I hear is not important. And how I interpret it—which is—you can't understand."

They moved among the apartment buildings in the centre ring of the City. The eastern sky was shadowed. Once they paused. "*The Lord of the Flames*," Jon said.

"Even you can feel it."

Jon nodded. "Can you spot exactly where he is or who he's inhabiting?"

"Not yet."

They moved further through the growing buildings.

"What do you hear now?" Jon asked.

"I hear an Executive Supervisor of one of your father's plants wondering if the assassination of Chargill will eventually affect his salary. He's talking to his wife about it. In the basement of their house is a drunken old woman who has wandered through their cellar door which was accidentally left open. She is hiding in the corner from what she calls the 'jibbies'

which actually are memories of the beatings her
mother gave her when she was a little girl on the
mainland. Neither the supervisor nor the old woman
is aware of the other's existence. And even if he were
to go into his basement, find her, and drive her out, or
if she were to pick up the length of metal pipe in the
corner, climb the stairs, sneak into the living room
and bash his and his wife's brains out—she has killed
two people in her life already—there would still be
no awareness exchanged."

"*The Lord of the Flames*," Jon said again.

"We're closer by a good deal."

"Can you see what he's doing now?"

"Not yet," Arkor said. "But in front of the military ministry a policeman is standing, waiting for his
platoon and darkness. They are going to make a raid
on a bar in the Devil's Pot where a mali gang is
supposed to hang out." Now they passed by a man-
sion familiar to Jon. "There's your father," Arkor
said. "He's thinking of calling in his secretary and
writing a letter to the supply commandant at Telphar
expressing his good faith in the war effort with a
pledge for half a million units. What will the publicity
value of that be? he wonders."

"Does he think about either me or my sister?"

Arkor shook his head. They passed on making
their way closer and closer to the Royal Palace of
Toron. "*The Lord of the Flames*," said Arkor.

As night closed finally between the palace towers
they turned down the deserted avenue of the Oys-
ture. At last they turned under a stone arch and Jon
opened the lock with one of the old-fashioned keys still
used in the palace. In the corridor they passed a
niched statue of the late King Alsen, and turned up a
broad flight of marble steps. They reached the fifth

. floor of the living tower and stopped before the doors of the Duchess's suite. For these inner doors swung inward over the carpet.

Petra was standing by the curtained window, fingering a smoky crystal in a silver-chain at her neck and gazing down over the evening City. She turned to them as they entered. "You're back," she said, no smile on her face. "The *Lord of the Flames*, I can feel him as though he were in the room."

"He's in the palace," Arkor said.

"That close?" the Duchess asked. "Arkor, can you tell what's he's done this time?" I've been dissecting government reports for a week and I can't see any place where he might have stuck his finger in."

"Nothing comes through that clearly yet. Maybe he had something to do with Chargill's assassination?"

"It's possible," said Petra. "I can't throw any light on that either."

"You said he's in the palace," Jon said. "Which direction."

Arkor paused another moment. "There," he pointed.

They went to the door, turned down the hall past the now unoccupied rooms of the Queen Mother and past the other chambers for royal guests. Finally they mounted a short flight of stairs to a hallway lined on both sides with floodlit statues.

"We're going towards the throne room," Petra said.

"That's right," nodded Arkor.

The hall opened into one of the alcoves of the throne room. Heavy draperies sagged towards one another at the fifteen-foot windows. Slender isosceles triangles lapped the polished floor where the illumination slipped between the draperies.

"Wait," whispered Arkor. In the quarter darkness Jon and the Duchess saw his forehead crease. He pointed diagonally across the hall towards one of the many other shadowed alcoves.

"We'll spread out," whispered the Duchess. "Remember all we have to do is see him all together."

Petra moved off behind the columns to the left and Jon started to the right. Keeping in the shadows of the sea-scaped tapestries, he worked his way along the hall towards the empty throne.

Then a voice came, hollow, from across the floor. "What is it! Who's there . . ."

His eyes froze fast to the alcove.

"Who's there? I'll call the guards . . ." A white figure moved through one of the spears of light, turning uncertainly and calling. "Who's there . . . ?"

The King! Jon felt a twinge of recognition and moved away from the tapestries. At the same time Arkor and the Duchess stepped out of hiding. At first the King saw only the Duchess and said, "Petra. You gave me quite a scare. For a moment I thought that you—"

Then:

The green of beetles' wings . . . the red of polished carbuncle . . . a web of silver fire. Lightning split Jon's eyes and he plunged into blue smoke. His mind hurled the parsces.

He saw grey, great strips of grey, but tinged with lavender, some with red, others faint yellow, orange. It took him a moment to recognize that he was on a desert, opalescent under a dim, grey sky. A wind pulsed and the tints shifted; orange glinted green, red lightened to yellow, the bluish colour to his left deepened; and the grey gauzed over all, endless and rippling.

His tentacles slithered up his trunk. His roots stretched far into this sand, down to a stream of pure hydrofluoric acid, nourishing and cool. But here at the surface the thin atmosphere was cold, dry, and grey.

Three heat-sensitive slits in his husk registered the presence of two other cactuses near him. He rustled his tentacles again and they rustled back to him. *Watch out,* rustled one cactus (that was Arkor), *There he is . . .*

Another cactus (that was Petra) swayed, tentacles lisping over the sand.

Something raised its head behind a near dune. Three eyes blinked and drew back.

Jon let his feelers hang still.

Now the head, onyx black, raised once more and again the three eyes blinked. The lizard hissed; needle teeth rimmed a spongy gum. It hissed again, and glowing sand swirled before its mouth. On six black legs it climbed the dune, heading in Jon's direction.

Suddenly Jon lashed out and caught the beast around the neck. Rasping, it pulled back, but the tall plant that was Arkor bent forward and three lanky fronds circled the reptilian body. The Duchess snared two beating legs, and together as they all strained back, the hissing turned into a scream in the thin air. The black skin parted and blue oozed over the broken limbs, darkened the sand.

The scream sounded once more, then stopped as the throat caved in beneath crushing tentacles. *There . . .*

It was dark. Moist soil slipped by Jon's rough skin

as his boneless body muscled through the earth. There was a vibration to one side and above. (Yes, it was Petra's.) He angled his burrowing until he broke through the ground separating them and was burrowing beside her, their flanks in rippling contact.

Where's Arkor? Jon asked.

He's gone ahead to the temple.

Is he back in good grace with the priestess?

Apparently. She sent a summons for him a heat cycle ago.

His offence was very great, and perhaps she has not forgiven him yet. I wonder if she suspects what part we played in the scheme.

There was a shudder along the length of the great worm beside him. *I hope not,* she vibrated nervously. *Then we'll be in for it. All we can do is attend the end-of-cycle prayers and hope she makes no denouncement.*

Now, except for their identifying vibrations, they were silent as they pushed towards the temple and the end-of-cycle ceremony.

It was a pocket of soft mud kept moist by perfumed liquids syphoned from every corner of the subsurface world. Jon could sense the exotic odours even before the texture of the earth changed and he broke into the luxuriant silt. They coiled near the back, waiting while the other worms joined them, waiting for the prayers to begin.

At last when the mud was filled, the familiar vibrations of the priestess reached through the temple. She communicated to her congregation through an ingenious amplifying system composed of a pair of metal rings that circled the mud hole, and when she curled around them and spoke, her words carried over the entire volume.

Hail to the great Earth Goddess in whose food track we reside, she began the invocation. *May the mud be pliable always.*

May none under her protection bifurcate until he chooses, responded the congregation; and the prayers began.

At last the rituals ended and the priestess began the announcements. *We have good news for you, my fellows. A member of our herd who previously incurred our displeasure is with us once more.*

Jon felt among the vibrations a new, but familiar pattern. (Arkor, he realised, must have just entered the temple.) But at the same time he realised there was something else present, something that had been there much longer, but was suddenly pressing in on his awareness. With a shudder the length of his intestinal track he realized it was the *Lord of the Flames*. The Duchess twisted apprehensively beside him. *The Lord of the Flames*, she whispered, touching her flank to his. *It's the priestess!*

I know, he whispered back, as the priestess continued.

This apostate again with us engaged in a plot to end the custom of our cyclic sacrifice to the Earth Goddess of eleven newly bifurcated children, claiming that to drive them down into the earth until their bodies were shrivelled by the Great Central Heat was beneath our wormlike dignity. But he has come back, said the priestess warmly, *and for his crime of subversion he had agreed to sacrifice himself at the beginning of the next heat cycle, and with him will be sacrificed his two co-conspirators in the plot . . .*

They didn't even wait for the identification vibrations to be sounded over the ring-amplifier. Both leapt forward, slipping between the other worshippers, sliding through the temple mud. When they reached the priestess, however, the temple was in mayhem. Jon bumped into a sluggish body that was sending out Arkor's identity vibrations, but the form was flaccid. Of course, he must have been drugged and carried here against his will. But the *Lord of the Flames* . . . Jon leapt for the priestess and coiled around the body only to find she and Petra were already grappling. With his nether end he dragged Arkor towards them. The movement revived the worm a bit, but someone had coiled about the speaker rings and was crying, *Help! Help! The priestess is being murdered!*

Other muscular lengths fell into the struggle, but the *Lord of the Flames: There* . . .

Cataracts of blue gushed from the rocks. Geysers of orange billowed from the burning stones, whipped the dark sky. The fire was beautiful, and the only other light came from the three moons in their shifting triangle in the night.

Jon soared above the fire, exaltation contracting the muscles of his breast. The air beat through his waxed feathers. His whistling wing tips arced the night again and again as he rose. Heat fanned his soft underfeathers. Opening his beak, the breath over his larynx quivered to song. *Arkor,* he called, *Petra, where do you fly . . .?*

Even before he had completed his questions, Petra's voice sang, *I fly over the green flames where the copper burns, now to the yellow where sodium flames . . .*

From further away a third voice joined them, *Hydrocarbons lap currents through orange tides . . .*

From the hundreds of birds around him, two joined

him and together they rose through the thickening smoke until the air cooled their wings, beating like hearts, without stop, without rest. The music blended, melodies wove and unwove with one another.

Then cawing cut the smoky air.

Dark wings flapped among the golden. Viciously it tore up at passing underfeathers with a purple beak; swooping down, its scarlet talon struck at an upturned eye. As it beat through the cloud of birds, gold feathers fell, were caught up on a breeze, then dropped again singeing, charring, at last to burst into fire.

Follow, cried Petra.

We follow, cried Jon and Arkor.

Jon whirled and arrowed towards the marauder. His beak plunged among black feathers. Talons meshed with his own. Arkor was close above him, and the terrible flapping of Petra's wings hammered from below. Then Arkor's beak jabbed a glittering eye, and the great wings shook, then relaxed. They were so entangled that at first they were dragged down nearly a hundred feet before their frantic flapping caught the air. For one moment they held the body in the dusty heat. One wing still shivered uselessly. Then Jon released his hold at the same time as Petra and Arkor, and as they rose, the whirling body fell. They watched the shadow burst into livid fire.

The Lord of the Flames they sang, *there*. From the corpse smouldering on the rocks a final fire leapt. Then Jon caught one glimpse of movement, soaring from the ashes, heard one bright explosion of melody as this new beast ascended toward the flock, before blue smoke washed into his eyes, only to be swept away by lightning. He was bound in a web of silver fire, he was lost in the red of polished carbuncle, and before his eyes was the fading green of flickering beetles' wings.

Jon stood in the throne room, blinking. To his left he saw Petra and Arkor in the dim light. To his right, at the foot of the throne, one hand clutching the fluke of the gilded squid, was the white cloaked figure of the King sprawled on the polished steps. The other hand still moved over tile. Jon ran up to him and stopped beside him. "He's alive," he called back.

There was a clattering of footsteps. He looked up to see guards all around him, their power-blades poised. Someone turned on the throne room lights. Arkor and Petra stood among the guards. "All right, what happened to His Majesty?"

Jon was flustered, but the Duchess began quickly, "We're not sure. We heard him call out as we were coming towards the throne room. Then suddenly he ran across the floor and collapsed."

"He's alive," Jon repeated. "But you'd better get a doctor to him."

"Move away," the guard said, and Jon stepped back. "Who are you?" the guard demanded.

"I'm the King's cousin," the Duchess said, "and these are my guests."

The guard frowned. "You better return to your suite, Your Grace. And stay there till we get this straightened out," he added.

Just then another guard came from across the room. "Yes sir, he did get a chance to trip the cameras before anything happened."

"Fine," said the chief guard. He glanced from Petra to Jon and Arkor. "This place is combed with cameras, you know, that can be tripped from a dozen places." He waited for some reaction. There was none. "We'll develop these and see what happened. Please go to your rooms."

Jon, Arkor, and the Duchess left the throne room. As they reached the hall, Jon released a breath that he had been holding since his last, *he's alive*.

In their suite, the Duchess dropped into the chair with the wooden back carved like shell, and ran the fingers of both hands through her hair. "I suppose where they have cameras, they have microphones," she said, glancing around the room. Arkor walked to one wall on which was an underwater sea-scape in tones of orange and sienna. He leaned his palm against the right eye of a stylized octopus in battle with a whale. "Now they don't," he said. "Or at least they can't hear anything out of it. Actually they haven't even put a monitor on it yet." -

"Those cameras almost foiled us when we kidnapped Prince Let. Thank God this time there won't be anything to see." She turned to the giant now. "Arkor, did you get a chance to see what the *Lord of the Flames* did on this visit?"

"It was more difficult this time," Arkor said. "Human beings' minds are a bit harder to ferret things out of than the neo-neanderthals where he was hiding before."

"Well, could you tell anything?"

"I can tell who murdered Chargill."

"Who?"

"His Majesty."

"Do you know why?"

"That I'm not sure. But there was something else in his mind, something that . . ." Suddenly he turned. "Jon, do you remember when we were coming here, I caught your sister's thoughts, and I said that something seemed to be wrong? I said there was some kaleidoscopic image that I could get the pattern of, but not the meaning? Well that same pattern, that same image was in King Uske's mind too!"

They were silent a moment.

Then Jon asked, "What exactly does the similarity mean?"

"It means that they both know something, the same thing, and even feel the same way about it. But it's hidden, like something you learn and then try immediately to forget. It was a lot stronger in Uske's mind, but it was there in both. And it may have something to do with the *Lord of the Flames*."

"Well, then what is it doing in both of their minds?" asked the Duchess.

"That's a good question," Arkor said.

"We'll try it on Catham to see what he comes up with—along with about umpteen others . . ."

There was a knock on the door. At the Duchess's nod Jon opened it. The chief guard stepped in. "Your Grace, gentlemen, the films have been developed. You are free to go and come as you like, but you may be questioned later on."

"Has His Majesty said anything yet?" Petra asked.

The guard looked from under lowered brows. "His Majesty is dead." He turned abruptly, and Jon closed the door slowly after him.

"I guess," said Petra, "that dislodging the *Lord of the Flames* was more of a jolt than he could take." They were silent.

"It's all a healthy man could stand," said Arkor, "and the King was sickly all his life."

Petra placed her long fingers together. "Chargill dead at the King's instigation. Now the King dead through . . ." She didn't finish. "With all this war business streaming about, the government is going to go through quite a contortion. All the little functionaries will start to wiggle and squirm."

"Do you think anyone will try to use the Queen Mother as a rallying point?" asked Jon.

"I doubt it," Petra said. "She's safe in her padded room at the General Medical psyche-ward. I hope she's happy, too. It's a shame she broke down last year. I remember her once being a powerful personality who might well have done the empire good."

It was Arkor who said, "This means it's time for Prince Let to come back."

The Duchess nodded.

"Just who is in line for the throne, I mean after Let?" Jon wanted to know.

"I am," Petra said, shortly. "You and Arkor must start out to the mainland forests this evening and bring him back as fast as possible."

"If we can find him in the forest."

"We'll find him," Arkor said.

Jon pulled back the curtain at the window and looked over the lights of the city, to where the sea spread like black cloth to a moonlit horizon. The transit-ribbon threaded from the palace, streaked with moon-silver, supported by mammoth pylons. The two-hundred-and-twenty-five-mile antenna beamed matter around the world. "I don't know," he said. "I wonder now if this is getting out of hand. No one meant to kill—or at least I certainly didn't mean to kill—the King."

"Are you suggesting that I did?" asked Petra quietly. "Ask Arkor if that was my intention."

"No, I won't ask," Jon said. "When I was in prison, I wanted . . ." He stopped.

"Jon, who was responsible for your going to prison?"

"Three years ago I would have said King Uske. But both of us were only children in school when it happened. Yes, something very twisted and sadistic made him dare me to break into the palace and steal the Royal Herald. But something equally foolish and headstrong made me go along with it, frightened me so much I actually killed the guard who was trying to stop me. But when I found out the King was dead just now, I waited for the feeling inside me, wondering whether it would be a sense of completed revenge, relief, or freedom. And it was nothing, I'm still not free, not just of the Triple Being, but of something in myself."

"Everyone has that," Petra began. Then she added more softly, "Perhaps you have it more than most, Jon Koshar."

Without turning from the window, Jon asked, "All right Arkor, you can sense it. Tell me what it is."

Arkor's voice, though not sad, came with a grave emotion Jon had not heard in his voice before: "I can't, Jon Koshar. It's another mask I can't pierce. It's easily the most familiar pattern that I see in your men's minds, almost the identifying mark of a human."

Jon turned from the window, sharply. "Guilt?" he asked. "Is that what it seems to you? Well now I perceive something very finely, and it's not guilt, Arkor. It's something . . . else."

The giant's eyes narrowed in momentary concentration, and when he spoke this time, it was with an uncertainty as new in his voice as the previous grave emotion: "No . . .it is not guilt."

Jon turned to the window again. "I don't understand," he said. "Perhaps Catham was right. Every time we exorcise the *Lord of the Flames* and suddenly go hopping around the universe, I wonder. . ."

"Wonder what?" asked the Duchess.

"I wonder whether this whole thing isn't a psychotic fantasy after all."

The Duchess drew a breath, giving her mind time to disengage from Jon's words. "I only know," she said, "that whatever this means, we can only act as we see. And we must return Prince Let to Toron as soon as possible."

Jon turned back to the room," All right. Then we will go to the forest and bring him back."

"Shall we leave tonight?" asked Arkor.

"Yes," said the Duchess. "I will try to get the council's ear and see if I can waylay some of the confusion that is going to result."

Jon and Arkor started for the door. A moment before they closed it, Jon repeated, with puzzlement in his voice, "A psychotic fantasy."

The Duchess looked up from the report she had begun.

"You have no time to worry about that," Arkor said to him briskly. "You only have enough to think it once, or perhaps twice, to convince yourself that it is not."

CHAPTER SIX

JERK A MAN from one world; fling him into another.

His boot soles hit the mud; he was in enemy territory; beyond the barrier. He hugged his arms tight around his chest and pulled against himself to release the excitement that quivered in his wrists and shoulders. The ground was as soft here as the swampy pools made by the sea's backwash in those winding inlets. The mist in front of him was as dense and damp as the autumn fogs that used to wrap his fishing boat at dawn. The air held October chill. And the sky, beyond the mist glowed faintly like the polished surfaces of well rubbed . . . shells . . . ?

No. Something wouldn't let him think that. You shouldn't think of that. Tel walked forward, trying to see. He felt vaguely unsteady, like the time when he had been lost for six hours in the dinghy one foggy morning when the oar had slipped into the sea. For a moment the mist gave way and he glimpsed the barracks to which he was to report.

He ducked forward, noticing that the ground was firmer, and at last stepped through the door of the shack. "Hello?" he called. There were no lights. He sniffed the fog floating in the darkness. It had the faint odour of sea-weed. The familiarity made everything more real, vivid. Yet he was somewhere in a half-dead blister of the irradiated earth, on some protected scab on the wrecked crust of the earth. "Hello," he called again.

"Hello yourself," came back a familiar voice. A face rose, came forward, its features materialising through the haze. "So you made it out here," Ptorn said. The black eyes smiled down at him. "Good for you. Quite a trip, eh?"

"Yeah," said Tel. "You can say that again."

"I think that's your bed over there."

Tel moved inside. Along the wall he could just make out a row of cots. "Hey, where's the enemy in relation to us?" he asked. "And where's everybody else?"

"We're pretty well behind the line of fire," said Ptorn. "And the others will be here soon."

"Sure as hell can't see anything around here," Tel said, squinting towards the door again. "Some of them damned bastards might be hanging around, just sneak up behind you, and burn you out. How are you gonna know?"

Ptorn shrugged.

"Hey, boy!" A shadow filled the doorway.

"Hi," Tel said, not sure if he recognized the newcomer, even though the voice was familiar.

"Glad to see you made it too."

"Certainly looks like you came through all right," Tel said, still unsure of who it was. ". . . Shrimp? Oh, I thought it was you. How do you feel?"

"Damp," Shrimp said. "Smells like the inside of an old lobster pot."

"Just like home," Tel joked back.

Another shadow darkened the door. "Ugh. Can't see nothing up here."

"There's nothing to see, ape," Shrimp shot back across his shoulder as he went to his bed. He dropped on his back on the mattress. "That transit jump sure takes a hell of a lot out of you." He stretched himself, arched his back, then fell back to the bed. Springs squeaked. "Like rocks," Shrimp mumbled, closing his eyes. "When the enemy comes around, wake me, hear? But not for anything else."

"Hey, Tel," said Lug, stepping into the shack, "I'll play you a game of randy."

"I'll beat you," Tel warned him.

"I don't care," the neanderthal said. "I just want to play. Over here."

"All right," said Tel. "A couple of rounds."

Lug hunkered down in the doorway where the light was bright enough to see and spread a handful of centi-units on the boards. Tel leaned on the jamb watching him. Then he squatted too and helped arrange the coins in the randomax square.

Darkness slipped across his hands, and he and the neanderthal looked up. A forest guard stood before them. Tel squinted through the mist. He could make out nothing distinctive about the features save the yellow eyes.

"Move. I want to get inside." The voice was cold. If sound could have colour, thought Tel, then this voice would shine like oiled steel.

"Can't you step over?" Lug asked affably. "We just got them set—" Suddenly a lot of expressions went over Lug's face: they were all types of pleasure. "Hey, Quorl! You're up here too? You're the first person I've met from home. I'm glad to see—"

The booted foot shot out, Lug and Tel snapped

their hands back in time, the coins went skittering.

"What the . . ." began Lug. "Hey," he called into the cabin after the guard. "Quorl, what's the matter with you? You don't have no manners, you know that? If you were my size, I'd bust you—"

"Keep quiet, Lug, " Tel said. Something in that voice bespoke a tautness he did not want to cut. Remembering what he had said about perception, he wondered whether or not Lug felt it too.

"But I knew that guy in the forest." The neanderthal was gathering up the coins. "Quorl, he was my friend. But now he's acting just like an ape that ought to be pounded around a little." He made a disgusted sucking sound.

"Hey, you guys are new up here, right?"

The squat hulk of a neanderthal stepped into the doorway. Lug blinked.

"You guys are new?"

"That's right," said Ptorn from inside.

"Then come on," the neanderthal said. "I have to show you something."

Ptorn joined Lug and Tel as they followed the other man out. "My name is Illu," he introduced himself as he led them over the soft ground outside the cabin.

"What do you want to show us?" Tel asked.

"You'll see," said Illu. "We show it to everybody who comes here. It makes them feel better. Some of them, anyway."

"What is it?" It was Lug who asked now.

"You'll see," Illu repeated.

They entered a clearing among the cabins. A post was stuck in the ground at the centre. As they approached, Tel saw that there was a sign nailed to it, pointing into the fog:

TOROMON—THIS WAY HOME

"The Scout put this up," Illu said.

"The Scout?" asked Tel. "Who's that?"

"A forest guard in our cabin, named Quorl," Illu said. "He's the guy who came in just before I did." He looked at the sign. "Doesn't it make you feel better?"

Tel was puzzled. But Lug put his ham-like hands against the post and growled with satisfaction. "Ummm," he said, looking from Tel to Ptorn. "Now we know which way home is. That means we know where we are. That makes me feel better."

Illu grinned. "I told you. We show it to all you new people."

"Quorl put this up?" Lug asked. He thought for a moment. "That's like Quorl. Back in the forest, a lot of times he made me feel better. Why is he so funny acting though?"

Illu shrugged. "A lot of people act funny out here. After a while you just sort of accept it, when you've been here long enough."

"How long have you been out here?" Lug asked.

"Aw . . . too long." He spat in the mud. "You knew the Scout back home, huh? Tell me what's happening back home."

"It's all crazy," Lug said. "All everybody talks about is the war. Nothing but war."

Illu nodded. "And now you're in it yourself. The Scout is a pretty important guy up here. Tell me about Quorl when you knew him back in the forest."

"Well," said Lug, "he was certainly different from now . . ." And the two neanderthals, having struck up a friendship, wandered off together, leaving Ptorn and Tel.

"I wonder how he figured it out?" Tel said, looking at the sign up close.

"He must know his math," Ptorn said.

The split plank that formed the post was grey and weathered, and the grain was separating. The nails had rusted quickly in the damp, leaving brown rings around the heads, like the nails in the weather-beaten boards of his father's boat-house. He was about to say something, but before the words formed in his mouth, Ptorn nodded his head and said, "Yes, it does."

When they got back to the barracks, most of the beds were taken with soldiers already in the regiment. In the lightless cabin, the figures looked like shadows through the thick mist hanging even inside. Tel went to his bed. As he sat down, the figure on the bed next to him suddenly rolled over. "Hey, you're one of the new guys that's come to fill up the holes."

"What holes?" asked Tel.

"You know; replacements."

Tel couldn't make out the face and for a passing moment was reminded of one of the featureless voices that had issued from the loudspeakers during basic training.

"What happened to the others, the ones we're replacing?" Tel asked warily.

"You really want to know?" responded the shadow.

"Not really." Tel ran his palm across the blanket, to detect the texture of the weave. "Do your eyes ever get accustomed to all this fog?"

"No. But you do."

"How?"

"After a while you get used to being half blind."

"Oh. Just exactly what do you guys do here?" Tel wanted to know.

"Well," mused the bulky shadow, "it depends on what you've been trained for."

"I'm a maintenance mechanic for the 606-B. And I know the 605 pretty well too."

"Oh, then you won't have any problem here with finding something to do."

Tel grinned through fog and felt a glow of usefulness, a warm reassurance.

"I gotta get some sleep," the shadow said.

"Hey, just one more question." Tel lowered his voice. "What's with that big yellow-eyed guard?"

"You mean Quorl, the Scout?" the voice came back.

"Yeah, the one who put up the sign-post."

"How do you mean 'what's with' him?"

"Well," said Tel, "he acts sort of funny."

"Sure he does," replied the voice. "He's the Scout. You'd be funny too if you had to do what he does." The springs squeaked again as the figure turned over. "Look, talk to me some other time about it, soldier. I gotta get some sleep."

"Oh, yeah," said Tel. "Good night." He sat back on his cot, alone, looking this way and that through the murky cabin. He wondered what Quorl's function was; then he wondered who he was a replacement for. Maybe he should have asked what happened to the person he was replacing, but . . . He was glad there was work for a 606-B repair man. Very glad; because he could take it apart, put it together, replace any worn part, tell when the slip plates had too much oil, or when the plumb coils were about to give. If only he knew what . . . if he knew what it was . . . No. He must't think that. Instead he thought about how good it made him feel.

A few hours later, when Tel was wandering outside the barracks, he stopped, bent down, and looked at his boots. They were coated with mud to the ankles. As he stood up, sucking breath between his teeth, someone called, "Who's that?"

"Eh . . . Tel 211 BQ-T."

"Oh, hi. It's me, Lug."

"Hey there, ape. I thought you were a sergeant or something."

"Hell no," Lug said, solidifying in the mist as he came forward. "You surprised me too." He came only a bit above Tel's shoulder, but his smile showed through the haze.

"Did your friend Illu tell you anything about what's going on?"

Lug scratched his head and fell into step beside Tel. "I don't know if I understand it."

"What did he say?"

Lug brought his hands together in concentration and his craggy face furrowed. "First he says we're in front of the main line of enemy forces. We're part of a string of bases thirty miles in front of that line. But what Illu said is that they're afraid they'll circle us and attack from behind." He looked up puzzled at Tel.

"What don't you understand?"

"How can they attack us from behind if they're in front of a string, a line of bases?"

"Simple," Tel began. Then he paused, remembering what Ptorn had told him about perception. "Look, Lug, how long is a string?"

"Huh? I don't know."

"How far does a string run?"

"From one end to the other," said Lug, shrugging. "How long is that?"

"That's as long as it needs to be: from one end to

the other. Now suppose the enemy comes around the ends of the string. Won't they be behind us then?''

Lug pondered a moment. ''Oh. I guess they will. I hadn't thought of going around.'' They went on a few more steps. ''That means we're in some danger, or we may be huh?''

''I guess so,'' said Tel, feeling at once apprehensive and at the same time affably superior for having solved Lug's topological conundrum. Perhaps that was what Ptorn felt like towards him, he reflected. Examining his own feeling, he was relieved to find in it nothing that the ape might resent. ''Just by being here, we're in danger, Lug.''

''Yeah. We have an enemy beyond the barrier,'' Lug quoted. ''Only now we're beyond the barrier too.''

They were nearing a rise.

''Hey, rocks,'' said Lug, moving to place his hands on the broken surface. ''Makes me think of . . .'' He did not finish his sentence, and Tel remembered his own first thoughts about the colours behind the mist, putting them out of his mind as quickly as before. He folded his arms, leaned against the rocky wall, and gazed through the fog. ''What do you think we're looking at?''

''Nothing,'' answered Lug.

''Mist, fog, water vapour . . . nothing. Lug, what's it like where you come from?''

''You mean . . .'' Tel could sense the words came from deep in Lug's mind. ''. . . home?''

''Yeah. What was your home like?''

''Home,'' mused Lug, ''was . . . the place I lived.'' He turned to Tel and grinned. ''Yeah,'' he said. ''That was what was best about it. It was the place I lived!''

Tel laughed, and again wondered how his own insights seemed to Ptorn.

"And Mura," Lug's voice became quieter, "and Porm, and Kuag; those are the people I lived with. Porm," he explained, "was my daughter."

"You have a daughter?" He hoped his surprise did not come through the mist. "How old is she? How old are you?"

"She's four summers old," Lug said. "I'm nineteen winters."

From somewhere Tel remembered that the average age of the neo-neanderthals was forty-five. To think of your life so short must make things appear very different. Yet a daughter, a family. Someplace in him, like an efflorescent crystal, he felt respect growing for this condensed, alien image of himself. "What was your home like?" he asked again.

"It was in the forest," Lug said.

"What else?" asked Tel.

"It was in a broken stone building, a 'ruin' they called it. From before the Great Fire. The big trees had pushed most of the buildings down, and there were stairs that led up and just stopped over open air. Children played with rocks and sticks on the stairs, and sometimes the wind came and we all went inside the stone building and stayed in the corner, and sometimes sang to the wind; or when the water fell from the sky, we sang to the water. When it was very hot, we danced for the sun." He stepped back and began to raise one foot and then the other with a little hop. "Like that, only with lots more people, and faster, with beating and shouting. Once a month we did that for the moon, only different. That's because the moon and the sun are different, and not like rain and wind. You understand?"

"I understand," Tel said.

"Sometimes we'd mend the leather over the hole in the sunward wall. But then you have to go out and catch a boar, or an elott—and outside, that's not home anymore. That's . . ." He paused.

"The rest of the wide world," Tel supplied.

"Yes," said Lug, screwing up his eyebrows and nodding. "And it's very, very wide, you know. Very wide."

Now Tel nodded.

"The rest of the wide world," repeated Lug. "That's very different from home. That's something else entirely. Home . . ." He paused once more, and at last took refuge in his previous revelation. "Home is where I live." Suddenly Lug grinned slyly. "All you very tall, very wise men who can get around the ends of strings, you must think this is silly. You must know where home is."

"Do you think it's silly?"

"No," said Lug, "but . . ."

"Then don't worry about it," said Tel. "It just may not be silly after all."

Lug pondered, then seemed satisfied. Now he moved back from the wall again and did his little dance. He stopped and looked up. "No sun," he said. "No moon. Home is where I live, and then there is the rest of the wide world. But where is this?" He gazed forward through the mist. "No-place."

Tel looked down at Lug's boots. "Don't your feet get muddy?" he asked. Because their big toes were comparatively opposable, the neanderthals felt uncomfortable in boots that prevented them from picking up things with their feet.

"They are too muddy," Lug said, wriggling his toes in the soft earth, "I wash them."

"I guess that's the way it goes," Tel shrugged.

"What's your home like?" Lug asked. "Is it the place you live?"

"It isn't," Tel said. "At least I haven't lived there for a long time, almost three years. I left when I was fourteen and went to Toron."

"Some of my people go there," Lug said. "I don't know if they like it very much. Those that come back say it's very complicated."

"It is," Tel said.

"What did you do in the City?"

"Just knocked around," Tel answered evasively. "Got into trouble here, got out of it there, couldn't get a job because there weren't enough jobs to go around, and ended up in the army." They leaned back against the rocks once more. "Say, did Illu say anything to you about your friend Quorl?"

"The guard who put up the sign-post?"

"That's right. And kicked up our game."

"Oh, the one with no manners. He's not my friend no more. All I know is he's a real important person around here. I don't know what he does, though."

"Maybe he goes out spying on the enemy. That's what I'd guess from the name. I wonder if he knows what the enemy looks like."

"You know you're right," said Lug, his face furrowing. "How are we gonna fight them if we wouldn't even recognize one if it came up to you and said hello?"

"We'd recognize it."

"Yeah." Lug said after a moment. "I guess we would."

CHAPTER SEVEN

ABOVE THE YACHT the stars were still. Water rushed the hull, whispering and lisping. At the horizon the jewelled towers of Toron diminished and sank down.

"Do you think after these three years that you'd recognize the Prince if he came up to you right now and said hello?" Jon asked Arkor. The wind was a cold palm against his cheek, cold fingers playing with his hair.

"I don't know," Arkor said. "His mind will have changed. His body will have grown."

Jon leaned into the wind, his eyes narrowing to pry between the two sheets of blackness, sky and sea, that joined before them. Finally he stood up. "Perhaps we'd better get some sleep," he said. "We'll be there by dawn." Together Jon and Arkor turned from the rail.

Sun broke through one layer after another of the night, till at last it burst bloody over the water. Already the shore was in sight. The forest came nearly to the beach. Once it had been an immigration port from the mainland to the island City. Now a burned dock sagged like a blackened limb into the tide, where a war plane had crashed there three years ago.

As Jon mounted the deck through the chill, he saw there were no other boats at the piers. Overhead a thin whine razored the sky. High above him, the sudden gleam of planes. They were army craft, carrying recruits from Toron to Telphar. The whine died, and he looked back towards the port which swung towards the boat through the lightening morning.

When Arkor joined him on deck, the wooden pilings were already thumping the side of the boat. The motor cut, reversed, and the space between the bow and the dock foamed with backwash.

A few dock-hands waited to catch the hawsers the crewmen tossed. One boatman appeared by Arkor's side, but the giant had already picked up the huge coil of rope. "I'll secure it," he said, dismissing the man, and flung the line across the closing slip.

They leapt ashore, Jon catching himself a moment by one of the near-rotten pilings, looking after Arkor who had already started towards the board walk.

A half hour later they stood among the trees. Arkor was listening, one brown hand against a barrel-thick oak.

"You're home now," Jon said. "What does it feel like?"

The giant shook his head. "Not what you think it should feel like." His eyes narrowed. "I don't hear anyone yet. Come on, let's go this way."

With surprising rapidity they made their way for the next hour through the forest. Abruptly the trees thinned, and in front of them Jon saw a glitter that must have been sun on the sea. They reached a cliff where broken rock spilled to ledges below. Fifty feet down, still a hundred feet above the water, was the largest table of rock. The sun burned white across the whole lithic expanse, and the small temple at the edge cast a sharp shadow.

"The priest is there," Arkor said. "Follow me down."

Before they reached the plateau, a man emerged from the door of the temple. Black robes caught the breeze shell hung by a leather strap over one shoulder. His face showed age more than any other guard Jon had ever seen.

"Why have you come back?" the priest asked.

"To take the young King to reign in Toron. His brother, King Uske, is dead."

"There are no kings in the forest," the priest said. "You have left us; why do you come back?"

Arkor was silent a moment. Then he said, "Three years ago, a young, light-haired boy came into the forest. He was the King's younger brother. The King is dead. He must rule now."

Jon noted that the priest was not marked with the triple scars of the telepath.

"Do you wish anything of him? Are you going to take anything from his mind? You know that is not allowed."

"I will take nothing from his mind," Arkor said. "His consent will be given, not taken."

"He is not of the forest people?"

"No," answered Arkor. "He came here and chose to avail himself of our people's hospitality. It is his right to choose to leave. May I have permission to search for him?"

The priest was silent for a space in which two

waves broke on the crumbling rocks a hundred feet below. "You may search for him along your own ways," the priest said, and turned back into the temple.

Jon and Arkor walked back to the trail that led up into the forest. "What was that all about?"

"How much of it did you understand?" Arkor asked. "I don't mean the words, but what was going on?"

"You were asking him for permission to look for Prince Let . . . and telling him why you came?"

"Yes, but I was doing a lot more." The giant hoisted himself up around a leaning sapling. "I was—how would you say it—acknowledging the status quo.

"It's like this," Arkor said as they gained level ground again. "Among the forest guards, the telepaths are in an ambiguous and uncomfortable position. In fact that was why I left. You see at once they are realised superior, and feared. It is understood that nature is aiming for the time when all guards will be born telepathic, yet the non-telepaths know that they are threatened by this growing minority. So the telepaths must be marked on discovery and must acknowledge the nominal sovereignty of the non-telepathic priest. It keeps peace and allows nature to go on."

"I hate to think what would happen if telepaths started appearing among us . . . men," Jon said. "There wouldn't be peace for long."

Arkor nodded. "That's why we keep the knowledge of our powers from you as much as possible."

"Occasionally I wish I could hear into other men's minds myself," said Jon.

Arkor laughed. "As I said before, it would be like

giving colour vision to a man still incapable of distin-
guishing one shape from another and who could not
even judge distances. It might be fun as a game at
first, but finally it would become a meaningless, an-
noying hindrance—to you."

Jon shrugged. "Where do we begin to look for
Let? It's your territory."

"First we find some people and check for any
knowledge of the boy."

"Is that what the priest meant when he said you
could search along your own ways?"

"That's right."

"Maybe your people are more civilized than we
are," Jon said.

At that Arkor laughed.

Like capillaries, a dozen paths threaded the body
of the forest. They had crossed nearly a dozen before
Jon recognized the subtle scattering of crushed
leaves on black earth, the broken twigs, the slight
compactness of the earth that marked the passage of
feet.

"Over there," said Arkor, "two women are nap-
ping on a cape of moss by the side of a fallen maple
log. One of them has seen the strange light-haired
boy with the limp, who is not of the forest people."
He looked at Jon. "It sounds like Let."

"Where did he get the limp from?" Jon wanted to
know.

Arkor shrugged. A bit later he paused again. "A
man passing by over there once hunted with the
light-haired boy. They made a moose trap together
six months ago."

Jon strained to see through the trees in the direction Arkor pointed, but he didn't even hear a rustle.

"In six months, Arkor, he could have wandered anywhere."

"True," said the giant. Suddenly he stopped short, and Jon drew up still beside him.

A moment later the leaves before them pushed aside and a tall guard with a shock of white hair running through the black at his temple stepped forward. Three scars ran down the left side of cheek and neck.

"You have come for the young stranger," said the guard.

"You know where he moves now," Arkor said. "You know that he walks by the high rocks, stops now, leans against the stick he is carrying and squints up at the sky through leaves like pale blue chips."

"You will follow the webbing of thought that holds him in the centre," said the guard with the white blazed hair. Without further interchange, Arkor continued walking in his direction and the other guard passed on in his.

"Now you know where Let is?" Jon asked.

Arkor nodded.

After a moment Jon said, "Why did you speak out loud?"

"We were being polite."

"You talk loud when you want to be polite to each other?"

Arkor glanced down at Jon. "We were being polite to you."

The light that lapped among the leaves grew yellower as day turned towards noon. Once they heard an animal screech in the distance, and once they walked over a damp stretch of ground through which a mazy stream delved in a rocky cleft. "There's something wrong," said Arkor after a bit.

"With the Prince?"

"No, not with Let, but with the thought pattern I'm following."

"What thought pattern?"

"It's like a radar net that all the telepaths, or most of them, maintain for directions, for information. You have to ask permission to use it. But there's something wrong with it, something down at the very end, dark, and unclear." He stopped and looked at Jon, his eyebrows pulling together. "And Jon, it looks for all the world like the pattern I saw in your sister and in the King."

"What's it doing here in the forest?" Jon asked. "Can you tell what it means now?"

Arkor shook his head. "The prince is through those trees," he said. "Perhaps you better speak to him first alone. It will recall things to him more quickly if a man presents them to him.

"Doesn't he remember?" Jon asked.

"It's been a long time, and he's young."

Jon nodded and stepped forward through the curtain of branches.

The figure turned abruptly and the light eyes narrowed in the dark face.

"Your Majesty?" Jon said.

The long, naturally fair hair was sun-bleached in uneven streaks.

"Your name is Let? You are the heir to the throne of Toromon?"

The figure stood very still. He held a staff in one brown hand and wore the garb of the forest guards, leather pants, a pelt across one shoulder for a cape. His feet were bare.

"Your Majesty?" Jon asked again.

The eyes widened now, extraordinarily bright in the

browned face. "Excuse . . . excuse me." The voice came rough, yet youthful. "If my speech is . . . slow. I haven't spoken much for a . . . long time."

Jon smiled. "Do you remember me? I and a friend brought you here three years ago. Now we are here to take you back with us. Do you remember, you were sent here by the Duchess of Petra?"

"Petra?" He paused, looking up now as if some answer would come from the trees. "My . . . cousin, Petra? The one who told me the story, about the prisoner who tried to escape. Only it wasn't a story, it was real . . ."

"That's right," Jon said. "I'm that prisoner."

"Why have you come?" the young man asked again.

"Your brother is dead. You must take over the throne."

"Did you know my brother?"

"Only a long time ago, before I went to prison." Jon paused. "I was just about as old as you are now."

"Oh," said the Prince. He took a few steps forward, and Jon noticed the slight limp. "There is a war on," said the Prince. "I hear them talk about it sometimes when they come to take people from the forest to fight the . . . enemy beyond the barrier. I will have to learn a lot, and there will be a lot to do. I remember now." As they went through the trees to where Arkor was waiting, Jon wondered at the speed with which the youth was adjusting to this new situation. Subtleties of perception, he reflected, wondering whether merely living among these people had caused any of it to affect the Prince. Arkor met them on the other side of the trees.

They had nearly reached the shore when Arkor suddenly stopped. "The boat!" he said.

"What is it?" Jon asked. They were still in the woods.

"It's malis," Arkor said, "at the docks, trying to sink the ship!"

"Out here, on the shore?" Jon asked. "For what? I just thought there were malis in the City."

"Gangs have sprung up all over Toromon. There's a forest guard with them, and the . . . the pattern I saw!"

Jon felt the momentary irony of the strange gang that had kidnapped the Prince and brought him to the forest three years past which Arkor had been part of. "Why are they wrecking it?" Jon asked. "Can you get any reason?"

Arkor shook his head. "The crewmen are fighting. One of them tries to start the motor, but a fire-blade slashes across his back and his scream goes all liquid and gurgly before he slumps over the control panel. Fire glints in the eyes of one man who jumps backward from the tilting deck as water sloshes across the boards and hisses against the fire. Smoke obscures the wheelhouse where the crewman lies." Arkor breathed heavily.

"Why?" Jon asked. "Why? Were they sent? Did they have a plan?"

"The malis," Arkor said softly, "the malcontents. No, or at least I couldn't detect any."

"What do we do now?" Let asked.

"We've got to get back some way," Jon said. "I guess we go in another direction."

The strain left the giant's face and he turned with them and nodded. They began to walk again, this time perpendicular to their original route. "We might be able to get back to the Island from one of the fishing villages, or perhaps catch a tetron tramp taking ore from the mines back to Toron." A bird chirped.

Once they came to a field in which a deserted farm house sagged into the slow breeze that waved across the riotous grain. Once more in the woods, night draped the trees until the moon rose and silvered the leaves. They came to another clearing where a great strutwork pylon soared into the air and a band of metal—the transit-ribbon—made a mark like a pen line across the lightened night sky. They slept at the edge of the clearing, and at dawn they continued.

In the brightening woods, Arkor heard the sound first. Then the two others stopped and listened. Beyond the trees, the tincan wail of a calliope sounded thinly through the morning . . .

CHAPTER EIGHT

"...THEN they started to fire on us from the left. We scrambled back behind those rock bags fast as cuttlefish. We must have splattered mud all the way back to Toromon. They have something that flames like the sun almighty and makes the fog look like powdered fire where it hits. A couple of times I've been to advanced platoons that have gone out to try and establish the beginnings of a permanent encampment but got messed up. It's pretty horrible what they do; nothing but pieces of guys all over the place. They'd told us this particular capture was going to be easy as cutting a kharba melon. They'd told us there probably wouldn't be a shot fired. Well I didn't want to end up like one of those gutted platoons and I swear I was about to take off over the rock bags and just beat it as fast as I could. Suddenly, though, there was a scrambling in the confusion of guys about twenty feet down the line. I remember I heard a rock bag fall, so I took a breath and figured—really sort of calm when you think how much sweating I was doing—'Well, they've finally broken into the fortress, and I guess I can expect to be dead in just about six seconds.' But I was wrong. The excitement down the line was growing. Apparently somebody from our side had scrambled back over the wall. Then someone turned on a hand-flood, and for a moment I saw a tall silhouette against the fog. Quorl had got back!

"I was down there in no seconds flat. Everybody else was crowding around too, trying to hear what he was saying. He squatted down in the mud and pulled the guy with the hand-flood down beside him. 'Shine it over here,' he whispered. We were all crouching to see. He began sketching in the soft mud, and you could just see where his finger scarred the ground with the dark and the mist. 'This is our wall,' he said. 'There's a nest here, and here. So they can hit us along the wall pretty hard. But remember, it's only two encampments. If you make a bee line fifteen degrees off twelve o'clock, you'll bypass both of them, and they won't be looking for you there. You've got about ten minutes before their next barrage. So get going.' He pointed over the wall. 'In that direction. It'll take you straight back to the base.' And before we could ask any questions, he was over the wall and gone in black fog. The next thing I know I was over the rocks running after the footsteps of the guy in front of me.''

"That was me," Illu grunted. "Running 'after', hell, you nearly ran me down."

The others laughed. They were sitting on a pile of boards that had been laid outside the barracks across the mud. Tel sat cross-legged, his back against the shack wall. Now he leaned forward on his knees to hear the rest of the story-teller's tale.

The fire had almost removed the immediate sense of mist, but along the curve of shacks he could see other fires blurred orange, curving away through the fog.

"That Scout," the narrator concluded from his seat atop the empty machinery crate, "He's a pretty good guy." Now he looked at Tel. "So don't mess with him too much. Yeah, he's a little strange, but . . ." The soldier shrugged. Someone else had asked the question, and Tel inside the cabin, hearing it start, had come out to listen.

Just then a darkness passed the fire near them in the haze. Then firelight touched the long neck, the open collar, the knifelike cheek bones, and the yellow eyes. Quorl swept his glance across them and he went straight into the shack. Shrimp, who was standing in the doorway, quietly moved aside. A moment later there was a creaking of bed springs.

"That's him," the story-teller said.

"He's really seen the enemy close up?" somebody asked.

The raconteur motioned for him to keep his voice down and answered softly, "Well if anybody has, it's him." He dropped his hands to his knees, leaned back in the darkness and yawned. "I'm turning in," he said. "It's just as hard to get up in the morning here as in Toromon."

Tel watched the group break up as some of the men from other barracks who had wandered over started back in the darkness. "Officers will be shooing us inside in a minute anyway," Illu grunted down to Tel.

"Guess so," Tel answered, stretched, and stood up on the boards.

He was just about to go inside when he heard a sound something between chirping, a cheeping, with a twitching melody beneath. It was coming from the other side of the barracks.

Tel stopped, glanced around the corner and held his breath. Something was beating the mud. Quickly Tel ducked back around the corner and grabbed the shoulder of the first person he saw still outside the hut. "Hey," he whispered. "There's something back there! You can hear it!"

"Probably a spy for the enemy." Then there was a laugh and the shoulder shook under Tel's hand. "Forget it, soldier. It's just one of the flip-flops that come around sometimes." Now Tel recognized the voice. It was the man who had the cot beside his.

"What are they?"

"Who knows, They're animals, I think. But they could be plants. They don't bother the enemy and and except for making noise, don't bother us."

"Oh," Tel said. "You're sure?"

"I'm sure."

The sounds came again, a distinct flapping sound, irregular, stuttering; then the chirping melody.

Tel went inside the barracks pulling his shirt out of his pants. He shrugged it down his arms, and sat on the edge of his bed. The sagging springs were tight against his buttocks, the air moist on his chin. He'd almost got used to the vegetative odour, but if he took the air deeply into his lungs, he could feel the rank smell far back on his pallate.

He pulled the blanket up from the mattress and slipped into the dark envelope with the warm spot from where he'd been sitting, listening to the sound the material made coming loose from its tucking, bringing a warmth to the surface of his mind by its familiarity. With his cheek pressed against his forearm, he squinted his eyes and listened. Outside in the mud he heard the flapping again, a sound like a loose canvas sail beating against a mast, like the slap of his mother's handloom when the treadles struck the leather stops and the threads shifted up and down, like his father's hand beating the water from his slicker as he strode up from the boat house, like his father's belt beating.

Flop-flip, flup-flep, flap-flep; he opened his eyes. The mist was bluish between himself and the barracks ceiling. He was lying on his back. It was very early in the morning. Flep-flap. The sound was just outside the door.

Suddenly Tel sat up, stuck his feet in his boots (the leather was damp) and stood up in his underwear. The mist was lighter now and the shadows on the beds were still. He went to the door and narrowed his eyes against the blue morning. Flip-flup. Last night's fire was dead, and the ashes and half burnt boards lay a few feet away. A very neurotic quail was walking among them.

Or maybe it was an extraordinary self-composed feather duster. It was exploring the remains of the fire on three large webbed feet. It poked at a bit of charcoal, circled it three times, then stood over it, squatted, and—injested it!

At first Tel thought he glimpsed a head or a tail, but no, the body was a shapeless ball of feathers. It flapped around another piece of charcoal, then changed its mind and sounded its chirping, whistling chuckle. Tel stooped at the doorway to look more closely. Perhaps the creature noticed him, because it cocked its head (body?), took six flop-flop steps towards him, then leaned its body (head?) the other way and did a couple of demi-pliés.

Tel laughed and the flup-flip twittered.

"Hey, what's that?" someone asked above him.

Tel looked up and saw Lug leaning against the door jamb, clawing at his hairy stomach where his undershirt didn't reach his underpants. Tel shrugged.

"He's sort of cute," Lug said. Then he coughed and ground his fist first into one eye then the other. "Damn mist," he muttered and spat across Tel into the mud. The flap-flip stepped back, then carefully waddled closer to the door. Tel held out his hand and made a rapid snapping sound with his fingers.

"Does it bite?" Lug asked.

"I'll find out in a minute."

At the sound the flep-flep leapt ten inches backwards, nearly lost its balance and began to plié again.

"Reveille hasn't rung yet. Why are you up?"

Both Tel and Lug turned quickly at the steel voice behind them. The Scout had come to the door. As he stepped forward the blue light slowly defined his equine features.

"Either shut up or go outside," Quorl said. "Men are trying to sleep in here, Lug. One or two of them even worked hard enough to deserve it." He stepped through the door, then looked back over his shoulder. "Go on. Get out of there if you're going to jabber." Then he glanced down and saw the flip-flap.

Tel and Lug had stepped outside and were standing uncomfortably by the wall when Quorl looked back at them, smiling. Tel met the smile with a puzzled frown.

Quorl pointed to the flop-flup who was now doing an arabesque with two of its legs, and perhaps listening. "Is that a friend of yours?"

"Huh?"

"Do you want a pet?"

Tel shrugged.

Quorl bent down, picked up a piece of charcoal and held it towards the flup-flop. The creature lowered its feet, scurried to Quorl's hand, straddled it, and squatted. Then it quietly wrapped its flippers around the Scout's wrist. As Quorl stood up, the flap-flop sagged over and dangled from his forearm like a feather pocket book.

"Hold out your arm," Quorl said.

Tel extended his arm alongside Quorl's and the forest guard began to flex his fist. The flop-flip suddenly got nervous and, one flipper at a time, transferred to Tel's arm.

"He likes charcoal and he likes warmth," Quorl said. "Give him both and he'll stay with you." Then he turned and strode off through the mist, buttoning his shirt.

"I wonder if he's going off to sneak a look at some enemy encampment," Lug said. "What are you gonna do with that thing?"

Tel looked at the flip-flep. Then the flop-flap did something. It opened an eye and looked back at Tel. The boy laughed out loud.

The eye was the milky hue of a polished shell, streaked with veins of gold. Another eye opened to reveal mother of pearl. Then a third (as the other two closed) shone through the feathers, streaked, like the first, but with red. "Will you look at that?" Tel said.

The third eye closed.

"At what?"

"Aw, it just stopped."

Lug yawned. "Let me get back inside and catch my last five minutes," he said. "I just got up to see what you were looking at anyway." He frowned after the Scout. Then he went back to the door and made his way to bed.

Tel raised the flop-flap and stared at it. Seven eyes appeared in the feathers; without pupils, their muted silver surfaces swirled with pastel lustres. A warm feeling uncoiled through him, fighting the coolness of the mist. He was beyond the barrier, gazing into friendly, familiar—so familiar pastel eyes.

That afternoon he checked over the 606-B. The asbestos washer on one clutch plate had worn down, so he stripped it as neatly as the rubber gasket would allow and took it to the quarter-master's station. He got a new one in under thirty seconds which was a relief after the time it took to get replacement parts on the training base back in Telephar. Once the flup-flup tipped the lubricant can and black oil spilled onto his arm and got all over his hand; after washing most of it off at the spiggot, he resigned himself to black-rimmed nails.

Once a tank rolled by close enough to reveal Shrimp riding in the open bubble. "How's it going?" Tel hailed him.

"I can almost turn this thing on a deci-unit," Shrimp called back.

"Good for you," Tel called.

"Hey, guess where I saw Curly. . . ." But the tank swerved away and the mist closed behind.

It was not until the knock-off whistle pierced the fog that Tel realized the flup-flup had left its perch on top of the assembly rack. Quickly he looked around.

Flap-flup came from somewhere behind him. He wiped his hands on the seat of his pants, turned, and started off through the mud. Once he hit a pot-hole, staggered, and nearly fell. When he got his balance he was just outside the semi-circle of cabins.

He listened and heard a twittering from the left. He turned and followed it. He had climbed over a three-foot wall of rock before it occurred to him that maybe it wasn't his flep-flop he was following. He stooped down and made the snapping sound with his fingers. Instantly the twittering began again, but still too far away for him to see. He took a few running steps forward and heard the sound of paddle feet receding. "Hey, come on," he called. "Come back and stay with me." Maybe he should have brought some charcoal. He'd put some in his pocket that morning, occasionally feeding the animal all afternoon. But now when he ran his hand into the envelope of his back pocket, the cloth was just gritty. "Come on back here," he called again.

Flep-flop, flip-flip, flop-flep.

He ran forward ten, fifteen, twenty steps. When he stopped the flup-flap stopped too and chuckled. "Oh, the hell with you," Tel said and turned around.

He walked maybe half a dozen long strides through the thicker mud before he slowed down and a frown deepened into his face. He turned right, took five steps, and stopped when a clump of leafless trees appeared before him. He frowned again and walked in the other direction. Five minutes later he noticed that the ground was extremely firm under his feet. He didn't remember crossing any ground of this consistency.

To his right the mist was bluer. He tried to recall: from which side had night approached the encampment? There was the grey afternoon, when he had met all the guys in the barracks. Then there was the night, sitting around the fire, listening to the stories the soldiers told. But how went the change between them?

He had started walking again when something brushed his cheek. He jumped and saw that he had walked blindly into another grove of spikey trees. The twig that had brushed his cheek had not been sharp and scratchy but wet; it bent like rubber. He rubbed his jaw, then reached out to touch the branch again.

Just then the idea of what being lost meant slipped into his brain and galvanised his spinal column, like a hot wire through his vertebrae. His hand drew back, and the rear of his thighs, his neck, and the small of his back felt like crinkled foil pulled slowly tight. He backed away from the skeletal trees. His legs felt soft, his joints all a-wash. The mist was thick and very close . . .

Something twittered on his left. Violently he turned right and ran. The mud splashed, and it was darker to his left. The ground was hard, then soft under his shoes. He ran. The mist clawed into his lungs and made the inside of his nostrils sting. He ran.

Then his hands snapped up just in time to keep him from crashing face first into a sudden rise of rock. He kept his cheek pressed against the veined stone, biting into tiny, terrified breaths for nearly three minutes, when he realised he was at the bottom of a cliff. The rock disappeared above him and faded away right and left. He turned his back to the wall at last and tried to keep his eyes closed and not think; but they kept on opening and darting about of their own volition. Hysterically they tried to fix on some form in the dark haze. Yet he was afraid to take his hands away from the rock behind him (where he had nearly rasped away his finger tips) and look at them for fear he wouldn't see them even if he held them in front of his eyes.

And something was coming towards him.

He mashed the air out of his lungs, his ribs strained like crushed springs. Mother, he thought, waiting for white fire; oh, mother, father . . .

"You pick a hell of a time to go off on a stroll," Quorl said. As Tel nearly collapsed from the wall, the forest guard's hand struck his chest sharply. "Breathe," Quorl said, in the dark.

Tel began to breathe. He wanted to cry, but choking down the rank damp air was more important. He peeled himself from the rock. The back of his shirt and pants were soaked.

"Don't fall down," Quorl said, "because I won't carry you."

Tel didn't fall.

"Come on. We don't have all night."

His legs didn't want to work. His first steps were irregular. "Where . . .where are we?"

"About forty yards from an enemy nest," came the slow, figuring voice.

That stopped Tel. "Wait a minute . . ." he managed to pant. "I thought they were . . . were thirty miles away. I couldn't have come that far."

"They don't wait for us to come to them. Get a move on. We're nowhere near safe."

"Wait a minute . . ." Tel got out again. "You mean they're really camped only . . . I mean you've seen them, really looked at them. You could take me close enough so I could look . . ."

"In this light with this mist," the Scout's polished voice came back, "you'd have to get awfully close to see anything." Then, with the same amusement in his voice as when he'd shown Tel how to coax the flap-flap, he said, "Do you want to go over and take a look?"

Tel had to clamp his jaw to keep from making the hysterical noise that ached and flooded up behind the prison of his teeth. All he did was shake his head. Whether Quorl sensed his answer, or actually saw his wagging head in the near black, his only words were, "Let's get going." Then, after a minute of silence, he added, "I've never seen them either." Finally the camp-fire glow pierced the mist ahead of them. Chills still raced Tel's back but he said, "Eh . . . thanks. What . . . made you come out after me?"

"You're a good mechanic. The 606-B is a pretty important machine."

"Yeah," said Tel. "I guess so."

As they passed the sign-post, there was a twittering chuckle, then a whistling chirp. Something went flep-flup by his left boot.

"It's been wandering around here all night trying to figure out where you were," Quorl said. "It's been lonesome."

"Huh?" said Tel. He stood still and blinked. Then he let his body drop to a stoop and extended his arm. The flip-flop's paddle-feet wrapped trustingly about his wrist.

"You mean to tell me you've been waiting here all this time? You mean you're just going to hang there and blink at me with those pretty eyes of yours and tell me you were here all along, while I was out running around in that . . . You ought to be ashamed of yourself! Why you ought to be ashamed!"

Like pure relief, like the upward thrust at the removal of pressure, the affection welled. And there were tears running down his cheek when he looked up.

Quorl had disappeared into the fog, by the barracks.

The nightly game of randy was breaking up. He fished a piece of warm charcoal out of the fire, fed the flop-flip, and set it to warm itself by the embers. "Man," said Illu when he saw Tel, "we thought you'd had it. What were you out looking for?"

"Just exploring," said Tel.

"Just don't explore yourself right into an enemy encampment. You know they've moved closer."

"Yeah," said Tel. "I heard."

When Tel got into bed, he was just about to go off to sleep when the soldier next to him raised up on his elbow and whispered, "You back alive?"

Tel laughed. "I guess I am."

The shadowed figure whistled. "I'm surprised. I admit it. You hear about the enemy moving in?"

"I know they moved."

"There may be a major blast soon."

"You mean a battle?"

"I don't mean a game of randy." Tel heard his head drop back to the pillow. "Well, good night, soldier. And I am glad to see you back, kid."

"Thanks," Tel told him, and rolled over. Outside, once, he heard the tiny whistling, chirping chuckle before exhaustion struck him into dark slumber.

CHAPTER NINE

FLAP-FLAP, flap-flap, flap-flap: in the breeze from the meadow, the canvas cover that she had pushed from the calliope beat against the back of the key-board console. Her notebook was open on the music rack and a strange graph of multiple lines waved over the page, cut here and there by single, double, and triple dashes. She struck a fourth, an augmented fifth. On the lower right hand corner of the page was a meticulous pencil drawing of a leaf. The model for the drawing had blown across the field and settled on top of the calliope bench for the eight minutes she had needed to trace its serried edge and fine veining, then tilted away on another gust.

She struck a third chord.

"What are you scribbling at?"

Clea turned, smiling. "Hello, Mr. Triton."

The rotund, bearded gentleman leaned against the console and looked back over the tents, wagons, aerial rides, and the metal runways between them. "Not too much business this afternoon. I remember when we'd travel through the farm lands here and have more yokels out than you could shake a stick at. When it came time for the Big Show you'd have to turn them away." He made a clicking sound with his teeth. "This war is a bad business. Still, we have an enemy beyond the barrier. What's all that scratching?"

"It's a new and totally useless method of musical notation. It's much too complicated for sight reading, though it's able to catch a lot more nuances in the music than the present system."

"I see," said Mr. Triton, burying one hand in his beard. With the other he began an arpeggio over the tinny notes. "I started out playing one of these things twenty-seven years ago." He took his hand from the keys and made a gesture over the entire park. "Now I own the whole thing myself." Then he let his arm fall and a disappointed look darkened the wrinkles already there. "This slack we're in, though; we've had slack seasons before, but never quite like this. We'll be heading back to Toron before the end of this week. At least there we'll be sure of a steady crowd. The war hasn't left people in the mood for circuses. And eyeryone's migrated to the city anyway."

Just then Clea looked over the top of the calliope wagon at the grassy meadow. Then she stood up.

"What is it?" Mr. Triton asked. "Who are they?"

Clea slipped out from behind the bench, jumped from the platform and began to run across the field. The warm stems brushed her legs. Once she ran through a clearing in the grain and from the yellow stubble, twenty locust snapped up before her. "Jon!" she cried. Stalks flicked her forearms.

"Clea!" He caught his sister in his arms and whirled her.

"Jon, what are *you* doing here?"

He set her down between them. Arkor and Let stood back.

"We came to pay you a visit. What are you doing?"

"So many things I couldn't begin to tell you. I've discovered a new overtone in the tetron vibration series. And did you know that the density of leaf veins, as they get further away from the stem is a constant, and a different constant for each leaf? You can put that in your useless information file. Then I'm working on something a lot bigger than all that, but I can't really go into it yet. Oh, and mornings I do the accounting." As they began to walk back towards the calliope wagon, she asked, "Who are your friends?"

"Arkor, this is my sister, Dr. Koshar. And this is . . ."

"Excuse me," Clea interrupted. "I'm travelling under an alias. They know me as Clea Rahsok."

Jon laughed. "We've got a secret too. Clea, this is His Royal Highness, Prince Let. We're taking him back to Toron for coronation."

Clea stopped and looked hard at Let. "It's possible," she said. "He was dead. At least that's the official information the News Service let out when he was kidnapped. You're still working with the Duchess Petra?"

"That's right."

"Oh," she said. "Well, come on and I'll introduce you to Mr. Triton."

"What sort of show have you got?"

"A good one," Clea said. "But no business." It was not until they had passed into the shadow of the calliope wagon that Clea stopped again and looked from Jon to Arkor. "Your eyes," she said. "Jon, can I talk to you later and ask some questions?" Then the volume of her voice raised as she looked up to the platform. "Mr. Triton, this is my brother Jon and two friends of his."

"Really?" asked Mr. Triton. "You don't say."

"We're travelling back to Toron along your route. We saw your poster up at the fishing village and decided to come by," Arkor volunteered. "It's a fine poster, too. It really catches your eye. Who designed it?"

Mr. Triton folded his hands over his belly, beamed, and said, "Why I did it myself. You like it? I even designed the mast head for the wagons back there. It's my circus from toupee to toe-nail."

"Would you show us around?" suggested Arkor.

"Well," said Mr. Triton. "Well. I believe I will. Come along. I believe I'll just do that." The flattered impressario climbed down the wagon steps and led them towards the tents, past the various stands and along the metal walkways.

A tongue of sunlight fell between the tent flaps. Jon stood just inside the door, breathing the warm odour of sawdust. Clea leaned against the dressing table.

"That isn't all your stuff, is it, sis?" He pointed to the open warbrobe.

"I share this dressing room with a friend of yours," she told him. "Now just what's going on, brother of mine?"

"I'll show you," he said, grabbing a piece of skin at his neck. He twisted it, and suddenly it tore loose. He peeled it upwards, and his jaw and half his neck and cheek came away. "You mean the acrobat. She's a good kid, Clea." He peeled away another slab of his face so that only the mouth and one eye socket were left. There was nothing underneath.

"I know she is," Clea said. "I wouldn't be here if it

wasn't for her. I asked her to tell me what was going on, once, but she said that the more people who knew, the more people who would be in danger. So I've let it lie. But I'm still curious."

The rest of Jon's face disappeared. "She was in a group, Clea, that today would go by the name of malis. I was a member too, you might say. Unfortunately we were marked, just like the forest guards you see with their triple scars. Our mark, though, was that we disappeared in dim light—like creatures of the imagination, if you will." He ran his fingers roughly through his hair which vanished as though a hanging wig had rubbed away. "Like psychotic fantasies," the headless voice came from above the empty collar.

Then his hand reached into his pocket, brought out a tiny capsule, and held it up to where his face should have been. The thumb pressed a tiny stud on one end and a fan of spray jetted out and caught the form of his skull, a transparent face, then swiftly opaque again.

"But there's a solution to everything." His face, though still wet, was almost complete again. "Now the job is to get a king back on the throne as soon as possible, and to end this war." The other end of the capsule produced a black spray which covered his hair. "Will you help us, Clea?"

"I'm impressed. But Alter showed me already," she said. "Maybe you can do an act in the side show. That stuff doesn't clog your pores?"

"No," explained Jon. "When it dries, it perforates and allows air and sweat to get through. But we've got to get Let back."

"Which faction are you working for?" she asked. "Or has the Duchess got her hand in for the throne herself?"

Jon shook his head. "Clea, it's bigger than any political hassling. It's even bigger than our enemy beyond the barrier; because we may have an ally among the stars."

Necklaces of light loop by tent and gambling stand. Couples stroll, eating fried fish from paper bags. A wonderwheel rings the darkness and children scuttle under the railings along the walks. At the bottom of the glass aquarium wagon, the octopus stretches over green rocks. The calliope hails notes against the neon night.

Alter came out the back exit of the big tent, lifting her white hair from the back of her neck with both hands. The breeze was cool across her nape and under her arms. She felt slightly light-headed from her bout on the trampoline before the applauding crowd. She ran down the passageway thick with clowns and sawdust.

She stopped when she saw the scarred giant. "Arkor?" she smiled. "How've you been? How's the Duchess, and Jon. And is there any word from Tel?"

"No word," he said. "But everybody's alive and kicking. Jon is here with me. So is Prince Let."

"You're taking him back to claim the throne? Good." She frowned. "What are you looking so hard at?"

"I'm listening." They had started walking beside the tent, Alter ducking under the slanting guy ropes, Arkor stepping over. "Alter, there's something in Clea's mind that I can't quite understand. It was the thing that was keeping her to herself. It was the thing that somehow you helped to break through. But I can't see it enough to understand it."

"It's Tomar," Alter said. "He was the soldier that she was engaged to at the very beginning of the war. And he died. She told me about it just before she got to work on this new project of hers. She says this one should be even more important than the matter-transmission projection."

Arkor shook his head. "It's not that, Alter. It's something much further down. It was something she figured out once and it was so terrible, she uses Tomar's death to avoid remembering the other thing. It has something to do with the *Lord of the Flames*, too."

"Clea?" asked Alter in surprise.

"As I said, I still don't know exactly what it is. But for one thing, all the telepathic forest guards also know about it, and they're using their combined forces to keep it away from me. They apparently know about my contact with the Triple Being and they're unsure of what to do about it. The information is in the minds of all the important councilmen, but the guards are protecting it in their minds. Clea seems to have figured it out all by herself, and then rejected it as too unbelievable. Alter, just listen to anything she has to say and see if something pops up."

"I thought I'd retired from this intrigue business," Alter said. "But I'll listen." Her fingers went to her throat to touch the leather necklace strung with polished shells.

Chains of lights dangle between tent and gambling stand. Couples stroll, crumbling their greasy bags. A merry-go-round whirls light over the hides of sea-horses and porpoises, and the children crawl from under the tent flaps again and scurry back to the walk-ways. Dolphins nose the corners of the aquarium wagons and the calliope plays faster.

"How do you like it, son?" Mr. Triton came up behind the blond boy in the forest dress who was leaning against a stay and looking up at the glittering trapeze act.

"It's fine," Let said. "I've never seen anything like that before."

"Never?" Mr. Triton ran his eyes over the boy's erect figure. From his height, he certainly wasn't a guard. "Well, then I guess it must be quite a sight for you." Beside them in the stands, the audience applauded.

"It must be hard to do that up there," said Let.

"It certainly is. But you know what the hardest thing of all is? It's managing all these people, each with his own individual act."

"How do you mean?"

"Well, I've done just about everything in this business, from play the damn calliope to training wild sharks." He paused and looked up at figures spinning in the aerial spot. "Come to think of it, I never was anything where I had to stay up in the air too long." Applause swept the dark tent once more. "But the hardest thing I ever did was trying to get them all to work together. You've got to listen to everybody's say, and try to keep everybody happy and alive at the same time."

"How do you do it?"

"You don't. At least never as well as you want to," Mr. Triton said. "You hold votes, sometimes; or sometimes you look ahead and put your foot down hard when there's disagreement. And when you're wrong, you admit it as fast as possible, and change to right if you can."

"Then what?" Let asked.

"Then you hope everything goes all right and that

you'll be around next season to hold your show."

The Prince looked up at the spinning artists. "They're beautiful," he said. "All that strength and delicacy at once; it's worth trying to keep that up there, isn't it."

"Yes," said Mr. Triton, folding his hands over his stomach. "Yes, it certainly is. You'd make a good circus person, boy."

Some of the lights have winked out by the side-show tent. The fried-fish wagon and the gambling stand, however, are still open. Couples stroll arm pressed against arm, hand in hand, head against shoulder. The bumper cars on the wooden arena still collide amidst laughter. The children stand on the walk-ways, knuckle their eyes and yawn. The manta-ray ruffles the sand at the bottom of the aquarium tanks, and the calliope player has stepped down from the wagon for chowder.

Clea decided to walk once more around the circus grounds before she went to bed. She passed the darkened sideshow tent and was going towards the wonder-wheel when she caught a look, or a feeling, she wasn't sure. She turned her head and saw the scarred giant who had come with her brother looking at her from about fifty feet away.

He looks like he's trying to see inside my head, she thought. Then she shook the thought away. Under everything she had been thinking of recently, was her new project. It was an amazingly beautiful, subtle, and profound unified field theory. It was far neater than any she knew—or would be when she finished it. It rose in towers of logic, plumbed oceans of reverberating overtones among syllogistic rhythms, and encompassed all her previous work on random spacial co-ordinates— ". . . gentlemen, it is more than conceivable that by converting the already extant transit-ribbon, we may send between two hundred and three hundred pounds of matter anywhere on the globe with a pin-point accuracy of microns."

No, don't think about it. Brush that thought away with the other. But you haven't thought about it for so long, so long . . .

And then she remembered his quiet smile, his bull-like body, the red hair, his sudden grin, and the inside laughter like a bear's. And then she stood, stunned, surprised, because the memory was so much clearer in mind, now, so that she did what she had never let herself do before, and whispered his name, "Tomar . . ." and waited for the pain that *should* come, only it didn't. Sometime in the last few months the wound had healed, and in healing he had not slipped away, but come closer, if only because she was in the world of life where he had lived, instead of the retreat world of death that was her own projection.

As she stood shocked motionless by the discovery, something from the deeps of her mind began to boil, to surge upward towards her consciousness, like a pattern clearing, a kaleidoscopic mayhem resolving into a recognizable, meaningful thought. . . .

No! She threw herself upon it, grappled with it, struggled to keep it out of her mind. No! No! Oh, please help me. No!

And . . .and . . .oblivion received it again.

She was panting, and the wonder-wheel, rimmed with lights circled the black. The calliope was playing again. She blinked, and looked at Arkor. She saw him frown once, shake his head slightly, and turn away.

The bulbs were black along the wires that dangled from tent to gambling stand. The couple threw a crumpled bag into a trash receptacle. The moon laid out a template of the wonder-wheel and the merry-go-around across the grass. The octopus, the porpoises, and the manta-ray had settled on the bottom of the tanks. The calliope was still.

They met by the darkened wonder-wheel, and the late moon turned her hair silver. Their eyes were hollow darknesses.

Jon smiled. "How do you like normal life now that you've lived it again for a bit?"

"You call a circus normal?" She smiled back. "How's it coming with the war? Will you stop it?"

"We've made another try at it. We chased the *Lord of the Flames* out of King Uske."

"What had he done this time?"

"We don't know yet," Jon said. "Clea knows. At least Arkor thinks she does. But it's too deep in her mind."

"That must be what he meant when he was talking to me earlier," said Alter. "How could Clea know, Jon?"

He shrugged. "It's not exactly 'know'; it's that she seems to have some obscure information that coincides with some that was in King Uske's mind when the *Lord of the Flames* left him."

"I see," she said. "You know, it's funny, I mean Tel and me. We're the only people in Toromon who really know anything about what you're really doing. And both of us have just sort of drifted away from it

all. He's in the army and I'm in the circus. He's off in
the war you're trying to end, and I'm . . . well, I'm
here." She dropped her head and then raised it again.
"I hope he gets back soon. I'd like to see him again.
Jon, have you got your own thing straightened out,
that search for freedom you used to talk about?"

"I won't have it until the war is over and I'm free of
the Triple Being. Or so I tell myself. In prison I
learned to wait. That's what I'm doing now. And
being able to walk around makes waiting a lot easier.
And I'm still learning things that will probably be
useful to me when it's all over. But sometimes I envy
you kids. I really do. I hope the both of you have a lot
of good luck."

"Thanks, Jon."

Before dawn the lights were wound up. The new
sun shone across the ballooning tents as they collapsed and were folded, then stacked at the side of
the dismantled gambling stand. A few children had
come to watch the wonder-wheel, the merry-go-
round, and the bumper-car arena dismantled. By six
thirty, the circus carts were rolling towards the shore
and the docks where the red and gold circus ship
would take them back to Toron.

CHAPTER TEN

THAT MORNING reveille sounded early. Tel gave the 606-B a thorough check before it was hauled off into the tank. Though the mist lay thick, the weather was warm.

"The King is dead."

"Huh?"

"In Toron, King Uske died at the palace. The report came through this morning!"

"Do you think it was an assassination?"

"I don't know. I didn't see the report."

The rumour washed over the camp like a wave. Though no one could be sure, it was assumed that the King's death had something to do with this sudden move they were making. And it was comforting, if only because it established some reason.

Tel was coming from the supply cabin with a number-three plumbing coil for the 605 (nobody had ordered him to, but he'd checked it on his own and found the number three nearly burned through) when he saw Illu carrying something over his shoulder. "What's that?" he hailed the neanderthal.

"It's the sign-post," Illu said. "I asked Quorl if he was taking it with us, and he said, 'What for?' and walked away. So I'm bringing it."

"Good for you," Tel said.

When he got back to the 605, he had to argue with the two guys who had just come to take it away and who didn't want to give him time to fix the coil. But then one of them saw the flup-flep and said, "Hey, you must be the fellow that they been talking about that's got one of them things for a pet." And during the time they were fooling around with the feathered animal, Tel got the coil in place. Then they went off, wheeling the 605 in front of them on a bearing-dolly.

When he was on his way back to the barracks, he passed Ptorn and Quorl at the corner of the cabin. "Perhaps this battle will be the final one," Ptorn said. "You mentioned there was talk of a truce?"

"Of a victory or a truce," said the Scout, "now that the King is dead."

Inside the shack, Tel was reaching under his bed for his rucksack when someone said, "Well, it looks like this is it."

"Huh?" said Tel, looking up.

The mist hid the man sitting on the next bed.

"Oh, how are you?" Tel grinned. "I guess there's no way to know where we'll be assigned in our next camp. I wish we'd gotten a chance to talk some." Tel gave an embarrassed chuckle which the other man returned.

"You heard anything about a truce?" the man asked.

"Just rumours. Do you think they'll end the war?"

The man shrugged.

"Well, I have to get to my departure detail. I hope we run into each other again some day." He picked up his sack and slogged out into the mud. He could hear the wheezing tanks lining up at the other end of the encampment. His order-plate said he should report to tank number three.

He was wondering if he would have any problem taking flap-flep along when a familiar voice called, "Hey." Shrimp solidified in front of him. "Tel? Yeah, I thought it was you." There was someone else with him. "Tel, here's Curly. How do you like that."

"Oh, hi," Tel said, shaking hands.

"How've you been?" Curly asked. "I'm over in Camp D-2. You guys working any good randy deals?"

"Hell no," Shrimp interjected. "Everybody in this camp's honest." He shifted his weight. "Hey, Tel, we were having a little argument about you. And we wondered if you'd help straighten it out for us, if you don't mind."

"Sure," Tel said. "What is it?"

"Just exactly what colour are your eyes?"

Tel drew his eye-brows together and shifted uncomfortably. "Green," he said. "Why?" And then wished he hadn't.

"Can we take a look?"

"I . . . I guess so."

Shrimp came very close to him and Curly looked over his shoulder.

"See, I told you," Shrimp said. "They're green, just like mine. That's cause we both come from the shore. On the shore almost everybody's eyes are green—"

"That's not what I meant," said Curly. "What I'm talking about only happens when it was darker, and not as much light as now. Come on, let's get in the shade."

"Hey, look," said Tel, "I gotta get going. I'm supposed to be at my tank and ready to pull out."

"What tank do you take?"

"Eh . . . three."

"Good. That's the one I'm driving. Come on."

Tel jutted his mind out in five different directions for an escape but struck brick at the end of each; so he walked with them through the fog towards the dark row of tanks.

"Here's my baby," Shrimp said, whacking the black metal hull. It rang hollowly as they went around to the side.

"Inside'll do it," Curly said, opening the door. The hydraulic ladder dropped its rubber casters into the mud. "Now I'll show you what I mean."

Tel mounted to the tank behind Shrimp and in front of Curly.

"No, don't turn on the light. That's the whole point."

In the three-quarter dark tank whose only illumination came from the pilot bubble at the other end, Tel stood against the wall while Shrimp and Curly peered into his eyes. Tel's heart was going like snapped fingers.

"All right," Shrimp said. "Now what colour does that look like to you?"

Curly frowned. "I don't understand it," he said. "Back in basic training, whenever it was half dark, they always used to look like they just weren't there."

"But . . .but my eyes are green," Tel said. Something was turning inside him, like a smoky crystal full of memories he could not see. "My eyes are green."

"Of course his eyes are green," Shrimp said. "What other colour would the eyes of a fisherman be, or the eyes of the son of a fisherman."

"Yeah. I guess so," Curly said. He looked again. "They're green all right. Maybe I'm crazy."

Yes, thought Tel, my eyes are green, always have been, and always will, and wondered why he had felt so nervous when they had asked to look. Why should they be any other colour, he wondered. Why?

"The King is really dead back home?"

"Yeah. I heard it at the report office. Do you think that means the war may be over soon?"

"Who knows. They say this is going to be the big battle. Maybe this will decide it."

"I hope so. I'd give my eye-teeth to get back to Toron, hell, just to see what it looks like."

"Me too."

As the tank whined through the mud, the mist struck in gusts against the oval portals. Tel sat at the end of the bench. In the bubble-seat at the front, Shrimp jogged right and left, his hand on the steering rod, his head and shoulder in silhouette on the fog. They had been going for an hour when there was a sudden burst of sound of their left, like rocks smashing.

The men looked at each other. "What was that?" someone called up to the driver.

Shrimp shrugged.

The rising and falling of the tetron motor sizzled beneath them. Tel leaned his head back on the wall. The vibrations had nearly put him to sleep when there was another crash. He came awake to see light flare through the right window.

"What the hell was that?" somebody bellowed. "Are we under attack?"

"Shut up," Shrimp called from the driver's seat. "Shut up back there."

Then, through the instruction speaker in the

corner, a voice came: "Be calm, alert, remember your training. Drivers proceed as scheduled. Stand by for orders."

Tel waited, trying to pull down the beating blood that filled his body. The tank rolled forward.

Half an hour later someone said, "This is a hell of a way to fight a war, all trapped up in a damn clam-crate."

"Shut-up," the officer with them said.

The flep-flap was sitting quietly under the bench. Now Tel reached down and gave it a piece of char-coal. As he bent forward and his cuff pulled up, feathers brushed his wrist.

The next time he looked at the oval windows, it was getting dark. They had been going a long time.

"All drivers halt," said the speaker.

Shrimp's shoulder jerked as he jammed on the brake stick. The tank lurched. Tel reached under the bench and set the bundle of feathers on his lap. All its eyes were tightly closed.

The men began to scrape their boots back and forth over the floor. The benches squeaked. "Come on, relax," the officer said. "You guys'll get your chance."

"Convoy disembark," came through the speaker.

The men stood up, stretched their legs, and punched at the ceiling to stretch their arms.

The door clinked open, the ladder dropped, and Tel, in his turn, climbed out. Except that the mist was darker and thicker, it might have been the same place they had left. As the group at the ladder's foot grew, Tel noticed that the ground was a little firmer here. Just then there was a crashing noise through the evening.

Their eyes snapped left; fire, fifty feet away, rose white and billowing through the mist. A momentary silhouette of spiky trees—

Suddenly there were orders breaking in the air all around them. "Tank-four to your left." Despatch convoy report to Major Stanton." "Convoy from tank three follow me."

Tel followed at a half run as they left the tank. Two men joined them from another platoon. Suddenly they were stopped, the group split in half, and Tel was herded off left while the others went right.

They had just passed a group of tanks when there was another hit, this time on the far side. Tel squinted. Heads turned as the deep blue evening flamed, then darkened. "Throw those rock bags up!" someone was calling. "Throw those rock bags up!"

Tel turned in time. A heavy burlap sack scraped into his palms, yanking at his shoulders. It nearly pulled him to the ground. A man on the other side was waiting for it, and Tel tossed it on, turned back, and caught another. They were making a chain of rocks across the area.

"You and you—" (neither one was Tel, but the order made him turn his head and almost miss a sack) "—climb that rise back there and report on D-T platoon."

Something metallic jingled to his left.

"Watch out! It's prickly!"

Three men were unrolling barbed wire over the rockbags. Coils spiralled over the burlap. The flip-flup jumped back just in time to avoid being stepped on and the coil rolled along the wall.

"Hey, you! They need you down the line about fifty feet."

Tel sprinted off. A handful of men, running to the

same destination, joined him when there was thunder and another flash. He clamped his eyes shut and nearly tripped over something. Someone steadied him and as he looked up a voice said, ''Hold on there, Green-eyes.''

Curly was one of the men.

They were ordered after one another to a new section of the wall. The rhythm was working its way into his shoulders, his body: steady yourself, catch, swing around, and toss.

Splat! He'd been too self-confident. He was bending down to pick up the bag when somebody yelled, ''Get down!'' He went down onto his knees in the mud and clutched the sack. His lids turned orange in front of his eyes and he felt heat all along his right side. When it went away, he staggered up, and nearly tripped over Curly.

Curly grabbed his arm and together they went as fast as they could back up along the wall. Suddenly Curly pulled him into a depression in front of the rocks. The flop-flop rolled in after them and twittered. The fog was deep blue, but through it Tel saw the sweat on Curly's face. They were both panting.

Behind them was the whine of a tank shifting position, a coughing stutter, a sizzling hiss of tetron units, then silence. Twenty feet away some men were hauling a machine.

''Is that the 606-B they're setting up?'' Curly asked. ''I thought I heard it humming. That's your machine, isn't it?''

''Yeah, it is,'' said Tel, trying to catch his breath. ''But I don't think I could tell a tank from an electric razor right now.'' Another hit caught them to the left. They ducked, and then Curly raised his head and peered around. ''Looks like they're giving us hell,'' he whispered.

"I guess they are. What are you looking for?" Tel asked. "I can't see a thing."

Curly pulled back into the pit. "Just to see if anybody's real close." His voice was suddenly grave. "Hey, I . . . I want to explain something, well, I meant something about me. To you."

"Huh?" said Tel.

"I felt sort of funny with that business about your eyes today. So, I got to thinking. And I figured I might as well tell this to you, about me; like an apology."

Tel's first surprise turned over in his belly, and though unsure of what was on the other side, he said, "Yeah, I see."

Curly smeared a muddy hand across his forehead. "Damn," he said, with an embarrassed laugh.

"There used to be this guy, in this mali gang I ran with back in Toron. He wrote these strange poems. His name was Vol Nonik, a sort of funny guy. Anyway, I wish I was showing this to him, because then he'd make a poem out of it. But he couldn't get into the army because there was something funny with his back. So I guess you'll have to do . . ." He laughed again, then looked down at his hands. "You've never seen anybody do this before, have you?"

"Do what?"

"Look." Curly said. "At my hands. Look."

"I don't under—"

"We may not get out of this thing alive," Curly said. "So look at my hands!"

Tel gazed at the soldier's cupped palms.

They began to glow.

They were bluish at first through the fog, but then the blue became red, a red fire flickering in his hands, a ball of red fire glittering just above his palms, shot with green, suddenly yellow, "Look," Curly breathed. "You see . . ." The ball of light lengthened, became slendered, bifurcating at the bottom and top. The waist thinned, the head raised, fingers articulated themselves at the ends of tiny, flaming hands. She bent, miniature, and swayed on tip-toe, wavering on his palms. Blue, copper, and gold flames like pin-points raced her body. A breeze (Tel felt it on the back of his neck) and her hair, a bell of sparks, shimmered behind her. She raised her arms and whispered (a voice like the whisper of water over sand): "Curly, I love you. I love you, Curly, I love you . . ."

"Isn't she . . . beautiful . . ." Curly's own whisper came like two rasps against one another over the voice of the miniscule homuncula. Curly breathed deeply now, and she faded.

When Tel looked up from the muddy fingers. Curly was staring at him. "You ever see anyone do that before?"

Tel shook his head. "How . . . how do you do it?"

"I don't know," Curly said. "I . . . just do. I used to dream about her, before I came to the army. But once, I thought: what would happen if I just made her happen. And there she was, like you saw, in my hands. I never showed anyone else. But with all this . . ." He made a motion around them. ". . . I thought I ought to show it to someone. That's all." Suddenly he seemed embarrassed. "Well," he grunted.

Tel glanced at his pet; and the flup-flip's polished eyes were open, and he wondered if it too had seen the flaming girl, so vivid, so sparkling, so real.

The whine of a tank motor grew behind him. Suddenly Tel whirled in the mud, and saw the looming machine. "Get out of here!" he cried to Curly who looked flustered and then dived right. Tel scrambled left. The tank careened towards him, passed within inches. He whirled to stare at the moving side and staggered backwards; for one moment he was close enough to see through the bubble dome, the tall, yellow-eyed figure of Quorl at the steering rod. Then the tank was past him, crashed through the rock wall. Fog closed behind it and swirled into the gap in the wall.

What the hell's going on? Tel wondered. A bunch of people were running towards them. An officer's voice stopped them. "Get the hell on down the line! Are you waiting for them to come in after you?"

Tel was running again when the next hit came—not close enough to blind him, but not far enough away to ignore. He caught himself short in the middle of a breath. In the harsh light he saw against the wall, tangled in the barbed wire, Shrimp: His left side was charred black. The mud had kept the rest of his uniform from burning. There was very little of his left leg, only the burnt stick of his left arm, and one cheek looked like crinkled carbon paper. The remainder of his face was vividly recognizable. Aflame and panicked from a former hit, he must have tried to climb the wall, forgetting where he was going and fallen back into the tangles of . . .

Then the light went out, and Tel was still running. He wasn't breathing; perhaps his heart had stopped; but his feet kept beating down into the mud. It was too dark to see anything now, but on the screen of night before him, blinking on and off, was the after image of the glittering flakes of burnt uniform . . . the red of drying blood . . . a net of iron wire.

They did a lot of fighting after that. During one lull,

the first stories began to trickle back:

"Did you hear what happened about the Scout?"

"What?"

"He was in that tank."

"The one that went berserk and busted the damn blockade?"

"Yeah. And they found him. He'd driven the thing smack through our wall into an enemy nest. He just crushed the whole installation."

"What about him?"

"They said the tank exploded when it hit. He knew that nest was there and that they would get us if they weren't destroyed. He saved the whole company."

"He sure picked a hell of a way to get rid of them. Where's Quorl now?"

"Are you kidding? They found pieces of that tank over half a mile radius."

In the darkness Tel pressed his cheek against the wet burlap, feeling the gravel through the cloth, and listening to the flap-flip's feathers. They tickled the skin on the inside of his knuckles. He thought about Quorl, and Shrimp, and wondered why . . .

CHAPTER ELEVEN

"MISS RAHSOK! Where in the world have you been?" The woman with the headkerchief set down her garbage pail beside the stoop. "I'm so glad to see you. Isn't it all terribly exciting, the coronation and everything? You'll never know what I've been going through. I'm so upset I don't know what to do. You know how concerned I am about my daughter, Renna. I don't even know how to begin telling you . . ."

"Excuse me," Clea said, "I'm in an awful rush . . ."

". . . what happened. I actually managed to get a ticket to the Pre-Victory Ball the council gave last week in memory of His Majesty. That was just before Prince Let had been found. I had to lie myself perfectly green to that atrocious woman on the committee about why my daughter hadn't been sent a ticket through the regular debutante channels. But I got it, and we made the most beautiful dress, all white and silver. What girl wouldn't love a white and silver dress. It was gorgeous. Well, you would have thought she was going to a funeral, the way she moped around. Renna does a little drawing, nothing great mind you, but suddenly her pictures turned

completely morbid, skulls lying in the branches of
trees, dead birds, and one perfectly hideous little boy
crouched on the sand about to be swept away by a
wave. I should have known something was wrong
right then. She kept on saying she didn't really want
to go to the ball, she wasn't interested. Go for your
mother's sake, I told her. You may meet some Duke
or Baron, and who knows— Well, she thought that
was silly, and laughed. But anyway, at four o'clock
in the morning, she set off in her beautiful white and
silver dress. Oh, she looked so beautiful, Miss
Rahsok, I nearly cried. In fact I did cry, after she was
gone. She never came home. That evening I got a
letter that she had married that awful boy Vol Nonik I
told you about who writes poems and lives in the
Devil's Pot. Do you know he was even expelled from
the University? She invited me to visit them, but I
just couldn't go. She said that she would tell me
about the Ball, and that hadn't been so bad after all.
Imagine, a Pre-Victory Ball, not so bad: Isn't it awful?
Isn't it terrible." The woman drew up her shoulders.

"Excuse me," Clea said. "I'm sorry, but I've got
to get upstairs and get some things. Excuse me." She
hurried past the woman into the hall. Then she
slowed; she was trying to remember something about
the names Vol Nonik and Renna. Then she remembered when she had heard of the poet! She remembered his poem; she remembered Renna's picture.
Without resolving the memory, because it dated
from a time before those three discoveries, she hurried on.

She opened the thumb-print lock and stepped into
the apartment. The shutters were closed.
It's like a cave, she thought, where I spent so

much time. There's not enough room for an acrobat to turn a cartwheel, it's too dim to see the grease paint on a clown's face even if he were standing just across the room, and you can't hear any . . . any calliope music.

She had come back to pick up her notebook with the odd radical formulae she'd never thought she'd look at again. But then I never thought I would want to look at anything again, she reflected. She went to the desk, thinking of Alter, Mr. Triton, and all the red and gold that was the circus. As she opened the drawer, she rested her other hand on the desk, and her fingers brushed a crumpled piece of paper. She frowned, stood up, and spread out the sheet. Yellow letters blazed across green:

WE HAVE AN ENEMY BEYOND THE BARRIER

Viciously she tore the paper across, tore it across again. She flung the pieces into the waste basket, snatched up her notebook from the opened drawer, and left the apartment.

Around the corner of the hall from her, something crashed to the floor, bringing her up from the pit of unformulated anger. She ran forward to see what it was.

"Oh . . . oh. . . good morning, Miss Rahsok."

"Dr. Wental, it's three o'clock in the afternoon!" exclaimed Clea. "Isn't it sort of early to be . . . in this condition?"

The doctor raised his finger to his mouth. "Shhhh . . . I don't want my wife to know. I'm celebrating."

"What in the world are you celebrating?"

"The young King's coronation. What else?" As he tried to get to his feet, Clea took his arm. "Oh, the bars are filled to bur—(urp)—sting. Everyone's celebrating! The war will be over! The war will be over and all our boys will be back. Hold on a minute there, will you?" The doctor shook his head and steadied himself against the wall. "A new king, and a new age, I tell you. You have no idea how good an age it will be. But then, you have no idea how good an age it has been. Who knows where I'll go, what heights I'll have scaled . . ."

"What *are* you talking about?"

"My medical practice," said the doctor, and chuckled. "I get new recommendations every day, every day."

"Your lupus erythermatosis patient got better?"

"Eh . . . which one?"

"The first one, the one you had difficulty getting the medicine for."

"Him? Oh, him. He died. There was a very small stink about it, when someone accused me of not using the proper medicine or something. But they couldn't prove a thing. I have acquaintances on the Council; they couldn't prove a thing. The important part is that people heard about the recommendation, and every day, every day . . ."

"I think you can make it the rest of the way by yourself, Dr. Wental," Clea said.

"Oh, yes, of course. But when things go so well, sometimes you just have to break out and celebrate . . ."

"Not that door," Clea said. "The next one."

"Oh, thank you." He moved unsteadily to the next apartment entrance. "Yes, thank you so much. But be very quiet now, because I don't want my wife . . ."

Clea left him fumbling at the thumb-print lock.

The entertainers, supplied by Mr. Triton, were waiting in the palace garden for the festivities to start. Clea strolled over the plots of grass cut by stone walks, set with granite benches. Multicoloured canvas had been stretched over tent poles, and the circus people wandered back and forth in their spangled costumes, talking.

"Dr. Koshar?"

Clea turned to see the giant Arkor. "What is it?"

"We need your help."

"What do you want?"

"Some information." He paused. "Will you come with me?"

Warily she nodded.

"I don't want to frighten you," Arkor said. "And some of what I want to talk about will be frightening." They walked into the palace entrance. "Will you help us?"

"What do you want the information for? So far I haven't any idea what you're talking about."

"You do have an idea," Arkor corrected her. "Why else did you quit your government job three years ago, and shut yourself off from the world."

"Because I was unhappy, and confused."

"I know why you were unhappy," Arkor said. "What confused you?"

"I don't think I understand your distinction."

"The distinction was yours," Arkor said. "You have a very precise mind, and you usually mean what you say. I ask again, why were you confused?"

"You haven't answered my question," Clea said. "Why do you want this information?"

"Fair enough," Arkor said. "It's a piece of information that a number of people have, among them, most of the council, and the late King Uske. Many of

the people of the forest have it also. Yet it is being
protected very well. You are the only person we have
found who possesses this information who is outside
this protection.''

''You are being very imprecise,'' said Clea.
''You're going to have to be honest with me if you
want my help.''

''I said it would be frightening.''

''Go on.''

''First of all I can read your mind.'' He waited for a
moment and then went on. ''There are many telepaths among the forest guards. They have a constant
mental net that spreads all over Toromon. Now
though I can read minds, I have been excluded from
this net. I assumed it was because I was somewhat of
an apostate; my interests were not theirs, and among
the telepaths there is little . . .I suppose you would
call it nosiness. The piece of information I'm looking
for concerns the war, is perhaps the most important
thing about it, maybe the secret of ending it, of win-
ning it, or losing. The first thing that conceals it in
most minds is an incredible layer of guilt. I should
have been able to break through that, but I can't. It is
under the further protection of the telepathic net I
spoke of. I tried to get some explanation from my
people, in the forest, but though I was not discour-
aged from seeking along my own ways, I was given
no clue. You are the only person in whom I can detect
this information who is not under the protection of
the net. That's because you figured it out yourself
whereas these others have all been informed of it by
one another, and have had to deal with it somehow
on an official level. The guilt is there even more
strongly in you, but what I want is still there, glowing
beneath the surface of your mind.'' Arkor paused

one final time. "The last person we tried to explain any of this to insisted it was a psychotic fantasy. But he agreed to help us as though it were a hypothetical problem. So you have a positive precedent even if you don't believe me."

They turned down the hall.

"If I'm not being protected," Clea asked, "why haven't you dug it out of my mind already?"

"You're working on a unified field theory," Arkor said, "that you believe might be a great discovery; I have a great deal of respect for your opinions, Dr. Koshar. If I dug it out, it would leave your mind terribly shaken, and some of your creative faculties might be impaired. You'll have to fish it out yourself, with just a little prodding from me, and perhaps some verbal assistance as well."

"As a hypothetical problem," Clea said, "—and no, I don't know if this is real or not—" She smiled, "I'm game."

"Fine," said Arkor. "Now, as I said before, don't be frightened. But about an hour ago you tore up a piece of paper and threw it away, very angrily. Why?"

"How did you . . . I didn't tear." The confusion caught her with complete surprise. "Oh you mean . . . well, it was a stupid war poster, and I suppose . . ." Why was she so upset—

"Why are you upset now?"

"I'm not—I mean I just wondered how you knew I tore it—the paper, the poster—up. I was in my apartment with the door locked—"

"That's not what upset you. Why did you bring the poster into your home in the first place?"

"Because . . . because I just don't like this whole war business in the first place. I don't like the idea of

our people dying beyond the barrier for—" She
stopped.

"For no reason?"

"No." She took two breaths. "For something I
did, something I discovered."

"I see," Arkor said. "And that's why you quit
your job?"

"I . . . yes. I felt responsible."

"Then why did you bring the poster into your
house in the first place? And why did you wait all this
time, until you were about to leave that house for
good, to tear it up?"

"I don't know. I was . . ."

". . . confused, yes. Now what confused you?"

". . . confused because I felt guilty. I felt somehow
responsible for . . ." Anger started somewhere. What
right had he—

"For the war? But we have an enemy beyond the
barrier, Dr. Koshar. You mean that you personally
felt responsible for this whole governmental and
economic flux that produced the war? You must
know that there were many more factors than just
your discovery at work."

"For personal reasons!"

"You mean the death of your fiancé, Major Tomar?"

"I mean for the death of my fiancé Major Tomar in
the war!"

Arkor waited a moment. Then he said, "I don't
believe you."

Clea looked up at him. "That's your privilege."

"Shall I tell you why?"

"I don't know whether I want to hear."

"When did Major Tomar die?"

"I don't think I want to talk about it!"

"He died in late spring three years ago on a mission to wreck the radiation generators just beyond Telphar. You didn't make your discovery of the inverse subtrigonometric functions and their application to random spacial co-ordinates until three months after he was dead. Major Tomar didn't die beyond the barrier. He died in military service here in Toromon. Now how could your discovery have had anything to do with his death?"

"But I was working for the government—"

"Dr. Koshar, if you were half a dozen other people—half a dozen other brillant people—you might be capable of falling into that sort of sentimentality. But you have a hard, resilient, supremely logical mind. You know that's not why you feel guilty . . ."

"I don't *know* why I feel guilty then!"

"Then answer these: why did you bring the poster into your house if you didn't *want* to be reminded of the war? And if you were angry, if you disagreed with this 'whole war business', why didn't you tear the poster up the day you peeled it so carefully from the fence? Why did you leave it crumpled on your desk for nearly a year and a half? What *were* you trying to remind yourself of, something you had discovered but couldn't, wouldn't believe; something that today you thought you wouldn't have to remind yourself of again; tear it up, jam it into the waste basket, push it out of your mind . . ."

"But there won't be any war now," she interrupted him. "Remind myself! There's a new King now! There'll be a truce declared, they'll all come back, and there won't be any . . ." She was talking very loudly, very fast, and they had nearly reached the throne room. There was nobody in the palace hall.

Light through a rotating window passed over a random pattern that caught Arkor's attention for just a second.

Clea looked shocked. Something had been prying at her mind; she had been resisting, pulling down. But as the pressure lifted a moment, her mind relaxed.

It happened. It surged from the bottom of her brain like a tide, a geyser, erupting into her consciousness as an undersea volcano throws off mud, sand, and steam. She fell against the wall and whispered. "The war . . ."

But Arkor had taken a step forward. It hit his mind almost as violently as it hit hers. He tried to crawl away from it. "But we'll win the war! We have an enemy beyond the barrier. But we can—" He turned right and left, dazzled, confused.

From the wall, Clea shrieked back, "What war! Oh, don't you see! *What war!*"

CHAPTER TWELVE

AMONG THE SOLDIERS, Illu pounded the signpost into the mud. "How do you know if it's pointing right?" someone asked.

Illu shrugged. "It don't really make much difference, does it."

Tel turned away with Ptorn beside him. The barrack cabins at the edge of the new encampment were dim and distant through fog.

"It's good to be camped again."

Tel looked around at the men in the mist. "Yeah," he said. "Makes you feel like you've got your feet on the . . ." He pulled his boot from the mud ". . . ground again."

Ptorn laughed.

"You know, I've been thinking. I've been thinking about it a long time, too."

"About what?" asked the guard.

"About the Scout."

"You and a lot of other people," Ptorn said, gesturing back to where the group of soldiers were breaking up around the sign. "What's your particular thought?"

"It's: 'Why?' "

"I can think of six 'whys' I'd like the answer to," said Ptorn. "Which one's yours?"

"Just why he did what he did: why he smashed that tank into the enemy nest to save us."

"That's a pretty good one. Maybe he figured that if somebody didn't do it, we'd all go up in flames."

"Maybe." Tel haunched his shoulders. "You know, I suppose I could understand it better if the whole regiment was made up of guards. But it wasn't."

Ptorn laughed. "Look," he said, "we're all the same phylum, same genus, same species. All histosents. That's not the part to wonder over."

"Well, I do," Tel said. "You guards live a completely different life from the rest of Toromon. But you're fighting here. What about the neanderthals? How did they adapt so fast?"

"Have you asked any of the apes about it?"

"I will," Tel said. After they had walked on a few more steps, he said again, "But I still don't know 'why'."

Someone was running towards them through the fog. He nearly bumped into them, steadied himself on Tel's shoulder, and cried. "A truce! Did you hear? They're crowning the new King and there's going to be a truce! We'll all be going home! We'll all be going back to Toromon!"

He took off towards a group of soldiers standing around the barrack's door. Tel and Ptorn looked at one another. The forest guard grinned. "We'll go back!" They turned and looked at Quorl's sign.

They were called in later, and as they stood around the little room, the speaker announced to them through the mist:

". . . does not go into effect until six o'clock this evening. Until then we are still at war. We are quite near several enemy encampments. There will be no wandering off base. Until the truce is actually consummated, the enemy's defence will be doubly active. Anyone who strays beyond the camp limit-line will be considered guilty of aggressive action. When the truce conditions are concluded, we will begin preparations for decamping."

First whispers, then talk, then laughter spread through the men. They burst from the door into the clearing. Somebody took his shirt off, knotted it, and flung it into the air. Somebody else fell down, laughing hysterically. There was a lot of running around, and more laughing, and some crying. Tel saw Lug coming out of the barracks.

"What is it?" the neanderthal called. "Huh? What's the matter?"

"What do you mean what's the matter?" Tel called back.

Lug came up rubbing his eyes. "What's everybody shouting about?"

"Where were you?" Tel asked. "Weren't you there for the announcement?"

"I was . . ." Lug rubbed his eyes again and looked—it was in the way he hunched his shoulders a little—embarrassed. "I was asleep."

"A truce!" Tel explained, getting excited all over again.

"Huh?" His fists fell slowly from his face. He shook his head. "Huh?"

"Lug, they signed the truce! The war's over!" He gave the neanderthal a playful whack. "Ape, how do you manage to sleep through something like that?"

"I was tired," Lug said. He looked up at Tel and

drew in the thick ropes of his brow. "The war's over?"

Tel nodded vigorously. "Finished, over, ended: don't you see everybody cheering and jumping around?"

Lug looked at the rollicking men. "That means we can go home?"

"That's right. Home."

Lug smiled and yawned. "That's good," he said with his eyes still closed. "That's good."

"Lug, what are you going to do when you get home?"

He shrugged his shoulders up; then, as they began to go down, an idea suddenly flooded up behind his broad face and burst out in words: "I know! I'm going to teach."

"Teach?" Tel asked.

"That's right," Lug said; excitement lifted his heavy features. "I'm going to teach them things."

"You mean your people in the ruins?"

"That's right. I learned a lot of things just coming here that they should know. Like how to write down talking. Quorl taught me to do that, before he . . . Well, he taught me; and to read it too."

"The Scout taught you to write?" Tel asked in amazement.

"That's right," Lug said. "I started to teach my woman, and my girl child, and the others. Now I can go back. And we could plant kharba fruits in rows where the land was clear instead of picking them wild. You can take care of them better and can have a lot more of them that way. I was talking to a guy who lives on one of the coastal farms and he said that's the way they do it there. I've leaned a lot of things. Some of them here, too. And if I teach, then everything will be better for us. Right?"

"Sure," said Tel.

"Hey," asked Lug, looking down at Tel's feathery, flippered pet that was slapping back and forth and twittering a few feet away, "will they let you take that thing back with you?"

"I don't know," Tel said. "I hadn't thought about it."

"Do you think he'd be happy back in Toromon? It isn't very muddy back there, is it."

"No, it isn't. I'd like to take him, though. I like him."

Lug squatted down and made the snapping sound with his fingers. The flep-flep waddled over the climbed onto his hand. Lug stroked the feathers and chuckled. "Maybe if you had two flip-flaps to keep each other company, it wouldn't be so bad. But one by itself would get lonely."

"I'd like to keep him around up until I go, anyway, even if I couldn't take him back. He can sort of wave good-bye to me just as I leave."

"That would be nice. Going home," Lug said. "I remember a nice thing about home." His thick fingers halted in the feathers. "Near the place where I lived, there was a mountain, and on the far side, at the bottom was a lake. Some people came there and began to build, houses, paths, docks on the lake."

"It sounds very nice," Tel said. He wondered why they were building.

"When it rained," Lug went on, "just before morning, there would be fog—not like this fog—but if you stood on the ledge and looked down the mountain, you could hardly see the water, until the dawn cut through to the lake. The fog hid everything they were making on the shore. But the centre of the lake was like gold fire." He sighed. "That was nice."

"I guess so."

"Quorl, when I knew him in the forest, he went with me there once. It's funny how he acted here in the army."

"You've been thinking about the Scout too?" Tel decided his curiosity about the building would not be answered right now.

"Yeah." Lug nodded. "I guess I have."

"Guess we all have," Tel said. "Say, Lug. You want to look after the beast for a bit? I'm going to check my tools and see if everything's ready to go back. It'll take me about half an hour to run through them all."

"I'll watch him," Lug said. Tel walked off towards one of the barracks, calling back over his shoulder: "Thanks a lot."

Tel had been blundering under what he'd thought was his bed for five minutes when it dawned on him he'd probably wandered into the wrong cabin. The arrangement of the barracks was a little different from the old camp and he still hadn't got it down right. As he got up, he nearly bumped into the figure of another soldier about to sit down on the next bed. "Oh, hey, I'm sorry," Tel began.

"That's okay, pal," the other soldier said. "Say, aren't you the guy who used to be in my cabin back in the other camp?"

Then Tel recognized the voice. "Yeah, that's right. Glad to run into you again. I thought you'd been transferred to another company. How've things been treating you since we moved?"

The figure shrugged.

In the darkness of the cabin they sat now on opposite beds. The fog had thickened. The soldier was still a faceless shadow to Tel's eyes.

"Fair, I guess." The shadow chuckled. "It hasn't been too bad."

"I guess if you got through this damn war you can't complain about too much. Isn't it great about the truce? What's the first thing you're gonna do after you get back to Toromon?"

The soldier let out a sigh. "I don't know if it's all that great. Maybe for you guys it is. But me? I really don't have anything to do when I get back. I was hoping it would go on a little longer. I used to be in company forty-four. Now that was a great company. It really was. Now I'm here. I'd just as soon go someplace else after this and fight a little more. This ain't a bad life. Just risky. And I guess for me the risk's just about over."

"Oh," Tel said, not quite understanding. "Well, what did you used to do back in Toromon?"

The shadowed head shook slowly. "You know, I don't remember. I've been away so long, somehow I just don't even remember."

Tel frowned as the figure lay back on the bed. He stood up and went outside, stepping over the burned out logs from last night's fire. He was just about to go into his own cabin, when somebody hailed him, "Hi there, Green-eyes?"

"Curly?"

"In person. All ready to leave?"

"Just about. I still gotta check my tools. Hey, Curly, I wanted to ask you about that thing you showed me—"

"Shhhh." Curly's forefinger sprang to his lips. "Somebody might hear you talking about it."

"I just wanted," Tel lowered his voice, "to know how you did it."

"Have you tried it yet?"

"No, but . . ."

"Well, then don't bother me." Curly's annoyance got cut off when somebody cried out halfway across the muddy flat: "Hey you, come back." There was a distant, double flop-flup, flup-flop: one was the tiny flippered feet, the other, the open-toed neanderthal boots.

"That's Lug!" Tel said. "He must be chasing my—"

The form was just visible thirty feet away and moving further off.

"Where does he think he's chasing it?" said Curly.

"Oh, hell," Tel said, "I forgot to tell him about the boundary!" He ran across the mud shouting. "Come back here, you stupid ape! Get back here!"

He caught up to Lug some forty feet outside the camp limit, grabbed his shoulder and whirled him around.

Lug looked surprised. "It got away, and I just—" he began to explain.

"Just get back as fast as you can run."

"But the truce . . ."

"It doesn't take effect until six o'clock and the enemy's doubled its watch. Get going." As they started back at a trot, Tel felt his first panic break and found relief in a flow of friendly abuse directed towards the neanderthal's jogging back. "I used to wonder why the Scout would break his neck for us guys. Maybe I should know now, but I'm damned if I do. Come on, move." Lug speeded up. Then Tel heard the sound of flippers at his feet. He stopped and dropped to a crouching position. "Well, there you are!" He held out his hand and snapped his fingers. "Come on, baby," Tel said, "you can have a nice piece of charcoal when we get back."

Lug who was already inside the boundary line turned around and called, "Hey, I thought you said run?"

"Come on," Tel called once more at the flap-flop who opened four shell polished, pastel eyes and blinked at him. "Come—"

That was the last sound he made.

Lug staggered backward from the thunder, his lids clamped shut before the column of white fire that spurted where a moment before Tel had crouched.

"What the hell was that?" someone cried from across the flat. Ptorn ran up and grabbled the neanderthal's arm. "Lug, what happened?"

"I don't know . . . I don't know—" His eyes were still closed and he was shaking his broad head back and forth.

One of the officers was shouting: "God damn it, this war isn't over yet! Now who was outside the boundary! Who was it?"

By the barrack wall, Curly looked up from his cupped hands where a flaming woman danced on his palms and frowned.

CHAPTER THIRTEEN

". . .PRONOUNCE YOU King Let of the Empire of Toromon."

Jon, standing in the first gallery below the raised throne, watched the councilman back away from the blond youth who was now King. There were not more than sixty persons in attendance: the twelve councilmen, members of the royal family, their guests, and several other important or highly honoured state personages. Jon was there as Petra's guest. Among the others was the grotesque imposing figure of Rolth Catham, the historian. The King paused while he looked over the people in the room, and then sat upon the throne.

Applause rippled among the participants.

A man in the back of the room looked over his shoulder at another noise, louder than the clapping. It came from the antechamber. Someone else turned, then still more people. The guard's attention was alerted by now. Jon and Petra both received mental nudges at the same time. "It's Arkor," Petra whispered, but Jon had already begun to make his way back through the guests. The Duchess paused just long enough to get Catham's attention, then followed.

When Jon pushed into the smaller chamber there was confusion. Guards were holding Arkor. Clea was leaning against the wall.

Arkor was saying calmly but loudly. "No, we're all right. Yes, thank you. We're all right. But we must speak with Her Grace."

The sentries looked, the council members stared. A moment later Jon saw the King push through the door with a guard on either side. "Now what's going on," one of the guards was demanding.

It was Petra who suggested the private meeting in the council room. The members sat along one side. At the head of the room the young King sat on a slightly raised chair. On the other side sat Jon, Petra, Arkor, Catham, and Clea.

"Now what is it you want to say?"

The Duchess nodded to Arkor who stood up and faced the council. "I have somebody here who is going to tell you something that you all know, but have insulated yourselves from. Something you all did, decided consciously was the only way out of a problem, but took that decision only at the assurance that you would not have to remember making it." He turned to Clea. "Now, will you tell the council what you were about to tell me, Dr. Koshar?"

Clea stood up. Her face was pale. "They won't believe it," she said. Then her voice grew firmer and she spoke directly to the council. "You won't believe it. But you know it anyway." She paused. "I spoke to many of you three years ago when I first made the discovery that enabled you to send people, equip-

ment, and supplies off to war. You were incredulous
then. And you will not believe this at all: there is no
war."

The council members looked at one another and
frowned.

"But . . ." spluttered one of the council members,
"then what . . . I mean where . . . are all our soldiers?"

"They are sitting—" she took a breath "—in tiny
metal cells stacked up like coffins in the vast section
of Telphar where recruit soldiers are not allowed."

"And what are they doing there?" demanded
another council member.

"They are dreaming your war, each one desper-
ately trying to dream his way back to what he knows
is reality, somewhere deep in his mind. Sodium pen-
tathol drugs keep them in a foggy, highly suggestive
state; three years of constant propaganda keep their
minds trained on the subject of war; six weeks of
basic training formally designed to make a psychotic
of the steadiest mind lends the final unquestionable
patina of reality to the dream in which every sensa-
tion of the real world, the sound of wrinkling sheets,
the glitter of sun on water, the feel of wet cloth, or the
smell of rotten wood, is fitted into a mosaic defined
by whatever each one fears and loves most, and is
called war. A computer with an information-sorting
mechanism that can take whole sensory patterns
from one brain and transpose them to another keeps
all these dreams co-ordinated with one another."

"Oh, that's ridiculous . . ."

"It's impossible . . ."

"I don't believe all this . . ."

It was as if the doubt released a mental flood gate.
It was as though Jon had suddenly acquired another

sense, sharp as sound or sight.

In terms of sight, it was like standing before a vast pattern of bright lights rising around him yet still before him. In terms of sound it was as if a symphony's opening phrase had begun and he was waiting for the cadence to resolve. In terms of touch, it was as if a storm of frozen and heated winds swirled towards him but had not yet stuck. But it was neither sight, nor sound, nor feeling; because he still felt the ridged back of his chair, could hear the rustling of the councillors' robes, and could see their worried faces, their narrowing eyes and pursing lips.

"Why did the telepathic guards protect this secret in their minds?"

The answer came back like fire-words, music, waves of tingling foam: Arkor said, "Because they did not know what else to do with it. It was an idea, this war, which sprouted in the late King's mind, yet the seeds of it are in every mind in Toromon. The one man who opposed the King, and that even after the plan was well under way, was Prime Minister Chargill, who was assassinated. They felt they could neither help nor hinder you in your effort because they did not understand it. The government asked their help in obliterating the knowledge from the minds of those officially connected with the project, and since it was a solution to the economic problem, they consented; because we could not refuse."

Jon and Petra both stood now beside Arkor. "Then understand our effort now," Jon said.

"Our intent was to save our country," said Petra.

"And to salvage the freedom of each man in it," said Jon, "freedom from such oppressive . . . dreams!"

"Then what must we do?" asked the collective

mentality of the telepathic guards.

"You must go into every mind in Toromon and
release the knowledge of war. You must band them to
one another for one moment, so that they both know
themselves and each other, whether they be in the
royal palace or the coffin-cells of Telphar, or the
stone ruins beyond. Do that, and you will have
served this breed of ape, man, and guard called Human."

"Some minds may not be ready."

"Do it."

There was a wave of consent.

And the doctor in the General Medical building
dropped his thermometer against the desk and
realized, as the mercury beaded over the white plastic, that his anger at the head nurse who always put
the progress tags on backwards was hiding his
knowledge of war;

Vol Nonik drinking at a Devil's Pot bar ran his
fingers around the wet ring his glass had left on the
stained wooden counter and saw his frustration at
being expelled from the University for "unbecoming
conduct" flogging him to ordered speech;

Councilman Rilum caught the thirty-year-old
memory that spun in his mind of the time that a
clothing industry that he had been vice co-ordinator
of had burned down, and realized his rage at the lax
enforcement of fire regulations;

A man who worked in the aquariums paused on his
way across the wharfs, took his hands out of his back
pockets, looked at the scars beneath the black hairs
on his forearm, and realized his fury at the woman

who had whipped him with an iron rod when he had been a child on a mainland farm;

Councilwoman Tilla caught a fold in her robe and squeezed it with her old fingers as she remembered the catastrophe at Letos Island where her father had been killed when she had gone to help him collect fossils as a girl, and realized that the child's fright had been hiding the adult's knowledge of war;

Captain Suptus stood on the bridge of a tetron-tramp that was pulling away from the dock, blinked his eyes against bright sunset, remembering how a man with white hair had stood up behind a desk in the office of a shipping company (another company than the one he worked for now) and sworn, "You'll never set foot on another ship as long as I am alive!" and suddenly understood his terror at that dozen-years-dead man;

A woman named Marla dived from the coastal rocks and felt the waters close her in a fist of shadows. The rims of her goggles pushed against her face, and in the last light she tore the oyster from the shale and soared towards the surface again. Sitting on the rocks a moment later she worried her knife between the crusty valves. Crack, scrape, crackle; and the tongue of flesh, without pearl, shone wetly in the blue evening. And for a moment she remembered another, larger oyster in which had lain an immense, milky sphere, that had rolled away from her fingers, across the edge of the rock, and dropped with a miniscule splash twelve feet into green water. And her stomach had caught in a furious knot, and in that knot were tied such anger, such frustration;

A forest guard stopped by a tree and pressed his palm against the rough bark, and remembered the morning seven years ago when he and two others had been sent to catch a girl who was to be marked as a telepath, and how she had fought him with silent, maniacal indignation, and how his momentary anger had risen, connecting with a score more of tiny streams;

A prisoner stepping from the mine-shaft lift spat in the footsteps of an overseer who had turned his back and was walking out into the ferns, then frowned, remembering her older brother years ago walking away from her down a dark hallway, and there had been tears running down her own face as she crouched in the corners; and she suddenly understood those tears;

Councilman Servin pressed his heel hard against the leg of his chair, glancing from one face to the other in the council room and thought: "Harsh, and uncomprehending, like my uncle's face the day he called me down from my room and in front of the whole family accused me of stealing wine from the green stall in the pantry, and even though I had done nothing, I was mute with fright, and was punished by being ignored completely by the whole family for a week and had to take my meals alone," and knew what had kept him from speaking then;

Across Toromon, a military recruiting officer suddenly lifted his pen from his paper at the same time, across the desk from him, the young neanderthal who had been about to mark the application raised his broad head, and the two stared at one another, each recognizing his own knowledge of war;

And in the palace garden, among clowns and ac-
robats, Alter sat on the ground against a marble urn.
Wind over grass and through leaves tugged at her
white hair. She moved her fingers along the leather
strands of her necklace, from the milky shell
streaked with gold, to the one that was plain mother
of pearl, then to the one with veins of red, and
thought, "Oh, he tried, he tried to dream some fragment of me into that terrible dream, dream himself
back into reality," as another had dreamed his
mother's face was always on the bottom of a certain
kind of rock, as another had been able to converse
with his dead father when the breeze made the leafless foliage shiver and speak to him, or as another
had found all beauty and love in a flaming figure
dancing on his fingers. "But he didn't know, he
didn't . . "

"How did you know?" Jon asked.

Clea moved her hand over the polished table-top
before she looked up at the council members. "Because I worked on the computer. Because I knew
from the reports on the conversion of the transit-
ribbon that progress couldn't be going that fast. Because there was a minor mistake in calculation in the
working condensation of the theory due to a typo-
graphical misprint that would have rendered the
whole process invalid and that no one ever caught
but me. Because I knew what the economic situation
of Toromon was, and I knew it had got into that bind
of great excess and little mobility that must mean
war. Because of a dozen things which meant this was
the only answer possible. Because it was assumed
that war would become such a reality in everyone's
mind that it would never be questioned; and because

they did not realize that reality must prove itself again and again to questioners, and that it is the fantasy which goes on without contradiction, without having to prove itself under logical rigour. The idea of asking questions was almost impossible; but only almost."

Rolth Catham stood up, sunset through the window striking the plastic case of his skull. "I have one more question, Dr. Koshar. How do the soldiers die?"

"Do you really want to know?" Clea asked. "Do you know the game randomax that has become so popular recently? The computer has a selector that works on a similar principal only with a much larger matrix, singling soldiers to be killed by random choice. Then, when the choice has been made, by controlled suggestion the dream is manoeuvred into some situation that will allow death. Then the cell in which the soldier is lying is electrified, his body is incinerated, and the cell is ready for another drugged madman who is prepared to fight the enemy beyond the barrier.

"Oh, the planning that must have gone into this," Clea said, "The probing and discovery. The complete slaughter of company forty-four with not one left alive, then the detailed report of the death of two men under the torture by the enemy. Simply turn them loose in the haze of their own injured psyches and they will create an enemy, greater and more malignant than any a psychologist could create for them, always hidden behind their own terror.

"They were stultified by horror, incapable of questioning law or reality, or any other facet of existence. Because after this training, the six weeks and before, no questions could be asked."

Catham raised his head slowly, and the young King stood up. "Perhaps," said King Let, "now, there will be peace."

Later they filed from the chamber to attend the coronation festivities. Jon started to turn down the stairway that would take him back to the garden when someone touched his shoulder. It was Catham.

"Yes?"

"I have some questions that are not for the rest of the Council," the historian said. "They're about your *Lord of the Flames*."

"Our psychotic fantasy?"

"If you will." The three-quarter smile formed on the human half of his face.

"Why don't you just rack him up to one of those elements of reality that must be questioned to prove the reality real."

Catham shrugged. "I already have. What I want to know is this: do you think the *Lord of the Flames* planted this monstrous idea of a war without an enemy in King Uske's mind?"

"Certainly not the idea," Jon said. "Perhaps the method for turning the idea into such a reality, though."

"I hope it worked the other way around," Catham said.

"Why?"

"Because of what it says about mankind if the idea *didn't* come from something extra-human." Catham nodded, and walked on down the corridor. Jon watched him go, then continued down the steps.

The circus people were all filing into the doorway of the palace auditorium.

Across the garden he saw his sister with her arm around Alter's shoulder. They stood quietly at the end of the line. He thought: *And what have I learned? Look, they all go softly into the doorway towards the spot-lights, even though they know now, the way they went before. Can I detect any difference in the way this one holds her shoulder up, that one has two fingers beneath his belt, the other fumbles with the gold braid on his chest? But what difference should there be? I have waited these years, I have watched. And I will still go pondering on what I have learned. Watcher and prisoner, I wait for freedom. At least from all this I know from which direction freedom will come; I have lived with my observation, and can at last move in to see what effect the observations have had on me. What can I salvage? Whatever is not clumsy and does not hide from war.*

The garden was empty now. Jon stood by himself in the swelling dark, fixed actor and observer in a matrix of matter and motivation.

And a universe away, a triple mind watched, ordered its own knowledge of war, and made ready.

SAMUEL R. DELANY

*04594 **Babel 17** $1.50

19683 **Einstein Intersection** $1.50

20571 **The Ballad of Beta2/Empire Star** $1.25

22642 **The Fall of the Towers** $1.95

39021 **Jewels of Aptor** 75¢

ROGER ZELAZNY

37468 **Isle of the Dead** $1.50

16704 **The Dream Master** $1.50

24903 **Four For Tomorrow** $1.50

80694 **This Immortal** $1.50

PHILIP JOSÉ FARMER

05360 **Behind the Walls of Terra** $1.25

78652 **The Stone God Awakens** $1.25

89238 **The Wind Whales of Ishmael** $1.25

Available wherever paperbacks are sold or use this coupon.

━ ━ ━ ━ ━ ━ ━ ━ ━ ━ ━ ━ ━ ━ ━

🔊 **ace books**, (Dept. MM) Box 576. Times Square Station New York. N.Y. 10036

Please send me titles checked above.

I enclose $. . . . . Add 35c handling fee per copy.

Name . . . .

Address . . . .

City. State. . . . . Zip. . . . .

44F

WINNER OF
THE HUGO AWARD
AND THE
NEBULA AWARD
FOR BEST
SCIENCE FICTION
NOVEL OF
THE YEAR

*04594 **Babel 17** Delany $1.50

*05476 **Best Science Fiction of the Year** Del Rey $1.25

06218 **The Big Time** Leiber $1.25

*10623 **City** Simak $1.75

16649 **The Dragon Masters** Vance $1.50

16704 **Dream Master** Zelazny $1.50

19683 **The Einstein Intersection** Delany $1.50

24903 **Four For Tomorrow** Zelazny $1.50

47071 **The Last Castle** Vance 95¢

47803 **Left Hand of Darkness** Leguin $1.95

72784 **Rite of Passage** Panshin $1.50

79173 **Swords and Deviltry** Leiber $1.50

80694 **This Immortal** Zelazny $1.50

Available wherever paperbacks are sold or use this coupon.